roxanne carter

GLAMOROUS FREAK

how i taught my dress to act

GLAMOROUS FREAK

how i taught my dress to act

roxanne carter

Jaded Ibis Press

sustainable literature by digital means™

an imprint of Jaded Ibis Productions U.S.A.

© 2012 copyright Roxanne Carter

First edition. All rights reserved.

ISBN-13: 978-1-937543-11-2

Library of Congress Control Number: 2012939082

Printed in the United States of America. No part of this book may
be used or reproduced in any manner whatsoever without written
permission from the publisher, except in the case of brief quotations
embodied in critical articles and reviews. For information please email:
questions@jadedibisproductions.com

Published by Jaded Ibis Press, *sustainable literature by digital means*™
An imprint of Jaded Ibis Productions, LLC, Seattle, WA USA
jadedibisproductions.com

Front and back covers and interior photography by Roxanne Carter.
Cover design by Debra Di Blasi.

This book is also available in full color, digital and fine art limited
editions. Visit our website for more information.

Beauty really has a lot to do with the way a person carries it off. When you see "beauty," it has to do with the place, with what they're wearing, what they're standing next to, what closet they're coming down the stairs from.

— Andy Warhol

TABLE OF CONTENTS

I. Beauty Is Quite Strange

ONE

As he laughs under his breath and cocks his head to the side, he's at once vulnerable and untouchable. Mythologizing himself, perpetuating rumors, *Everything you think is true*. Notes take shape – astrological symbols, secret messages received and encrypted in his own inscrutable language. *One a day, until I die*. At once extravagant and sublime, omens appear to him from a dream, a unicorn in a glade, two stars called Castor and Pollux heralding the highway, a slew of things tumbling from him propelled by their own strange locomotion. The natural boundless inventiveness of adolescents is his encyclopedic nest egg: he's perpetually pubescent, glistening with androgyne, not quite the rouge, vamping in black fringed boots, his ineffable grin sliding across my synapses. Otherwise innocent, inordinately shy, stripped-down in gold lamé.

He probably doesn't see me. I'm sure he didn't see me, standing there fawning, transfixed. Greed animates me; I flush with self-consciousness. Everything he says is suspect, can't be trusted. He deviously contradicts himself in the very instant I begin to believe. I lap it up, swooning after a quixotic vision in an ankle-grazing Edwardian frock coat. He's afraid to say too much, opting for too little, parsing each statement under the five-word limit. It's no trouble for him to answer pressing questions with sighs, to bite his lip, let slip one word clips, indecipherable rants against semiotics. Words wound him. He'd like everything to mean nothing, but be precious to everyone. He'd like his words to mean something to me. He tells me that afterwards I'll have something to think about. He smirks through boring interviews, looking out through the stadium dark directly into my eyes. Only my eyes. I'm sure he didn't look but it felt like it to me. It's unnerving, this suggestive, almost violent glance. I experience it as a first kiss, a demonic initiation. My flesh rises in response; his silence feeds my desire. He won't play by the rules, steadfast in his incredibly daring high heels and gold epaulets. He flits by several octaves, his upper register, the very limit, slamming down into my body and snaking out, euphoric. His hands on his hips. My equilibrium wrecked. *Tell me what to play*, he says, his doe eyes sliding over me. His bare chest, his hands cool and dry, manicured nails pressing into my skin. How will I call him, call him, call him? What will I say?

TWO

He notices me immediately. I lift myself, look back directly, back straight. I'm firmly suspended, exhilarated by the physical pleasure of knowing I'm admired. When he turns away a clap of cold strikes, a catastrophe. He needs his space. I feel abandoned, long to return to the carnality his eyes address, a liquid flush. The power of his gaze is unsustainable, but the lasting effect resonates in everything I do: waiting for the bus, sealing an envelope, a lyric courses and awakens me.

My uncertainty brings me closer to him: my face is near to his, but it's a closeness I can't complete, a static flickering on the television screen, stinging me. The telephone won't ring; it's busy, or offline. He might call and

I'll be holding, flipping channels, waiting for somebody to answer.

If I could keep up with all this pale glamour, subdued under a backlight, the microphone cord looped around his tender wrist. He draws taut, his face smug, his look pivots on me: I turn the dial. As this is happening, I have so much to do. The care of the house overwhelms me. There is no way to keep the walls clean. They need to be covered. He's truly possessed by a violence, which erupts – disturbing everything within his reach, although he remains sterile, impressively stoic. He carries himself well. How well? He knows his own quality, the ease with which he jerks.

I'm disturbed by my impulse to touch him. I may have actually called out. I'm so embarrassed… usually I'm not like this, willing to appear so ridiculous. *I'm flirting with everyone*, he says. I'll find a way to disrupt his disinterest; I'd be happy with one unraveling and illuminating word. As long as I have something to do, even sweeping the cat hair accumulated on the floor. I'm entirely concentrated on my determination, frequently and feverishly returning to the image of his leatherette, the fringe of metal swept across his forehead, the cuffs that bind him to the bed frame: they come to nothing. He has no secrets, and no opportunity to be released. He's on, on, on, a little different each time, hitting the bull's eye.

Where can I find him; what do I want from him? Action takes shape and dissolves desire. I'll say *yes* to anything. If I wait awhile this may snag, rewind. The mail might come. He is closed to me, unavailable. Only through repetition can I find access: here he is, rousing the timorous, opening the reserved. I could wear his face inside out. A beauty I want to devour, leaving nothing behind. He can't be exhausted: he's infinitely available, offering himself over and over again to everybody.

THREE

I like to watch.

His face caught in cameo, fixed on some unfamiliar distance, the black beetle of his eye framed by lashes gummed with ink. He nods to the beat, each thrust of his chin punctuated by a faltering withdrawal from his face – the stage which surrounds him extends from the edge out; within its confines he's unreservedly slim.

I don't know how this is supposed to be done. The spotlight singles him out; he's simply there, radiant in black and white. The elusive and unattainable dream to which he's open, which he invites — the mysterious transparency of his words give me a place to rest; I can settle, here, in the filth of weird beauty.

In the middle of willful exposures, the tails of his trench coat slap against his calves, the tops of his thigh high stockings barely meeting the shadow of his hip. These vague gestures are readable, and his adoption of recognizable signs collapse in a great clash; rococo motifs, jeans and neon overlap. The disparity of references brought into uneasy harmony: everything about him is right. On the word *Love!* his eyes roll up, the whites overcast. He has a multitude of meaningful looks. The artifice of his posture is so sincere that I find myself believing everything he says. He's so humble he can't help but mean every word — *love, love, love.* The vacuousness of repetition as suture. He animates his own performance, willfully leading me across the stage. I'll follow him; I'm willing to take any position, as long as I'm able to see. He struts to be seen, obscenely exceeding the limit of his own body, the stickiness of his whisper going right down through me.

I don't have to be beautiful but he is flawless, coiffed, buttressed by the allure of his tremoring lips. He knows he can make himself appear, half-on, half-off, and or not. I wish I wasn't up here alone. I'm open to his influence, and I'd like to be full, overtly fluid, excessive to the point of grotesque. My response is more intense the longer I watch, the more I hit play. I can't hesitate to use what I know; I've slipped in and I want to stay.

FOUR

I know that he'll die for me. I halt on a half-taken step, one heel hovering over a gleaming parquet floor. Overcome by jealousy of shadows, interrupted by light. He's given me the look; every feather singed, the coarse tulle of a veil curled at the ends, cauterized by fire. I extinguish the flame with my painted lips.

Birds move stiffly over water, wings spread to release. Everything burnished in black and white, a clean, chemical white that's artificial, dreamy. A white kitten, doused in cream. Women like love notes written on paper napkins, fluttering up against a flat, grey sea. The waves hurdling abandoned bouquets.

The glitter of kisses everywhere. He replicates himself in various ways: taking advantage of the gloss of a grand piano, mirrors that rise up as if from the earth, wavering to cull his reflection, his body swathed in extravagant ruffles, rosaries, ostrich plumes fawning over his bed. He never goes out without his face on, hair done, glittered to the hilt.

I'll keep an eye on him. He might be crashing my party, one curl plastered to his forehead. Not because he has to; he's here to have fun. I'm here; I've been here, home. I haven't been waiting but I'm checking him out. He gives me the look but what he's really looking at is the camera's gaze on him. He swells like a rooster; I'm cut from him, over here, longing to reach through. He wants to look, to own his image; I want more. Clearly, something has gotten into me; the full effect of his eyes has turned me inside out.

He can't help it.

He makes an effort to imitate the person he claims to be. This is the person he's become, doing the splits on top of a grand piano. The only way to keep something for himself is to continue to lie about it. He's always on the telephone, talking in a bedroom voice – silly and tender at once. I'm slightly nervous.

First, he'll touch himself, then me.

A ladder lies across the sand. At one end, a window. The other, the sea, pulling out. When he falls, I'll cover my face with my hands, lights flickering on bare rocks, a tendril of blood flowering from his half-parted lips.

FIVE

He said, *Now*, menacing. *Now now now*, a long way to go. *Now somebody is sending me roses!* He doesn't need to be marked by beauty. I really like him. I stood on my toes, the better to see him above the bodies all gathered at the foot of the stage. Never let him out of my sight.

He's so small I could've easily slipped him in my pocket and snuck him upstairs. His favorite way: alone. To be alone, slipping easily in and out. To please my mother I might have introduced him if I hadn't wanted him all to myself. Little Lord Fauntleroy on a Japanese motorbike. I'm the one with the eyes. With the yes. I'd call in late. We could have worn each other's clothes, although his high heels probably won't fit me. If only I wasn't so tall, so awkward, so hard to recognize among all these other girls. Whom I happen to resemble.

I'm home I'm home, he says, *is this my home?* Clicks his heels together, comes home with me. The dialogue is terrible. What can I say; I'll have to make some adjustments. I've purified myself in Lake Minnetonka. How his face has changed since he filled the screen. Admiring his own profile in the rushes. Drinking champagne out of martini glasses we laugh; always doing the wrong thing, laughing in order to appear honest. I had to laugh at the wrong moment – not like I was laughing at him. I'm a little nervous; I've already made an entry in my diary. He's a screamer OH DON'T STOP; when he's upset, he gets so silent I pull the curtains to cover myself. He struts across the stage, a strobe light thrusts and the dresses start to rip. All I've got left is this ruffle. What can I do with a ruffle, the set list, boys in high collars buttoned up with pearls, monkey fur and cockerel feathers? The click of his boots on the floor makes my heart want to settle down.

The more he fades the more perfect he is. The less he says the more I listen.

Anything he wants me to do; my hands wave limply above the crowd. Cassette tape in my hair, kiss, kiss to the camera. In sumptuous black and white, the stamp of his mouth marking me. He calls it glamour. As much as I know: he calls me a girl like a tall building, Godzilla girl, machine made and real. Is it me, really me he wants? We hardly know each other, though I know everything about him. *Did you see me?* he says.

Back to dancing, taping his photographs to my walls. Look how I feel, breathing deeply; sometimes I feel just like him. I can't help but be strange, difficult and fragile.

SIX

The radio was dead. Turning the dial, all he could find was handful of dashes. The discos were dead; the ladies were kinda dead; he'd started talking to himself. He made another body for himself and he called this body an altar, a servant of the temple. The body was in him and it had a girlish giggle. He lost two whole days; he had no call for sleep and so much to do.

He started with the word kiss and went from there. He made five smacking sounds with his lips and I try to copy him, standing alone in my room in front of the full-length mirror. I have a great many pretty things to blame him for. The mirror is all smudged with skin cells and I wouldn't mind if I just went broke. For a line or two, I speak the same as him. I've been accused of taking him all for myself.

As long as he can tell me as much as he can about what he does when he's alone in his room, I wouldn't mind. He says that an impulse calls him, a pinching hunger. He gets angry if he's disturbed and blazes as he takes his way. I won't be bothering him; I'll be engulfed in the business of the house, gathering the papers I've strewn around in a careless, confused manner. He can please himself by being deliberate but I'm not sure what I want to do today.

He's always catching up to me; I often can't go back to cleaning when a song I like comes on. Endeavoring to remove a stain from the stove, his softly spoken *No* will alter me. I'll end up strutting through the living room, a pulse going constantly inside, dispelling the dirty dishes.

SEVEN

Women are beautiful in a house. They look out of windows, their bodies slide effortlessly between archways, their cheekbones clang on lighting fixtures. Nothing will stop a woman from making a beautiful home, from becoming beautiful in a house, from becoming a house herself. Her legs will protrude from the doors, she will wear the house like a cocktail dress, she will lift her cigarette daintily to the gable-roof window, where her mouth waits. Now this is a dream. This is not actuality. A beautiful house, a man she loves living with beauty inside. She wants to see that his clothes are handsome. That he wears a hat, keeps his chin smooth, and carries a handkerchief, offering it to her when she sneezes, throwing it across puddles when she walks in her satin shoes. They're lost in this picture, a depiction of a home, a very beautiful thing. A woman… For instance, bouquets of flowers, shirtwaist dresses, costume jewelry, cake tins. All of these make living substantial. Her energy goes every which way… The freshly cut sunflowers and basket of newly fallen apples make a beautiful arrangement of the table. She's indifferent to etiquette, and when she's alone, she will eat in only her lavender slip, standing barefoot on a newspaper. She doesn't care. All right.

In the dining room, there's a beautifully set table. They had arranged it. They did this together. He exclaimed, *We did this together!* There are flowers, there are fruit. Here is a charming table, and what will it do? It immediately releases something in them to which they respond. Beauty is important. A woman has a beautiful life, a beautiful home; she lives with her head in the attic and knees pressed against the furnace in the basement. So firm, they blush. If it rains and there is a flood, the torrent will come, and take her in one gulp. She will not resist, so encumbered by architecture.

EIGHT

The quick, peculiar movements of her small hands. Rough answers made in bottles sealed with wax. Vessel after vessel tossed into the sea, left to wander rifts of water candied with ice.

Words come to her to be arranged, slips of paper erupting from her pockets, a corkscrew pressed against her thigh. She'll claim her own scoundrels, come home loaded with armfuls of objects limpid and flowery. Some sentiments she can't answer; lips have come together to set a stamp but she won't be struck. The stamp will not draw blood. She can't bring herself to keep a common sense. The things she wants back rarely wash up.

To see far-off land for the last time is to feel herself sinking. She comes from leafless forests, trees hung with tinsel and china birds, rude women clothed in lawn stitched with pine needles. Turn them and they drop, softened by a little distance. She looks towards the sea and receives its call, living all day in sand castles bricked with bottle caps, singing songs of her own composing, smiling to taunt the shade. She must remember her path, the passage of velvet gulls gliding in the sun.

Days pass upon the waves. Soiling her pale lips with offerings of clotted ink, a fragment learned from forests half-dismantled, captured in a bottle. She advances from the foothills decked in pearls, pollen clinging to her curling hair.

NINE

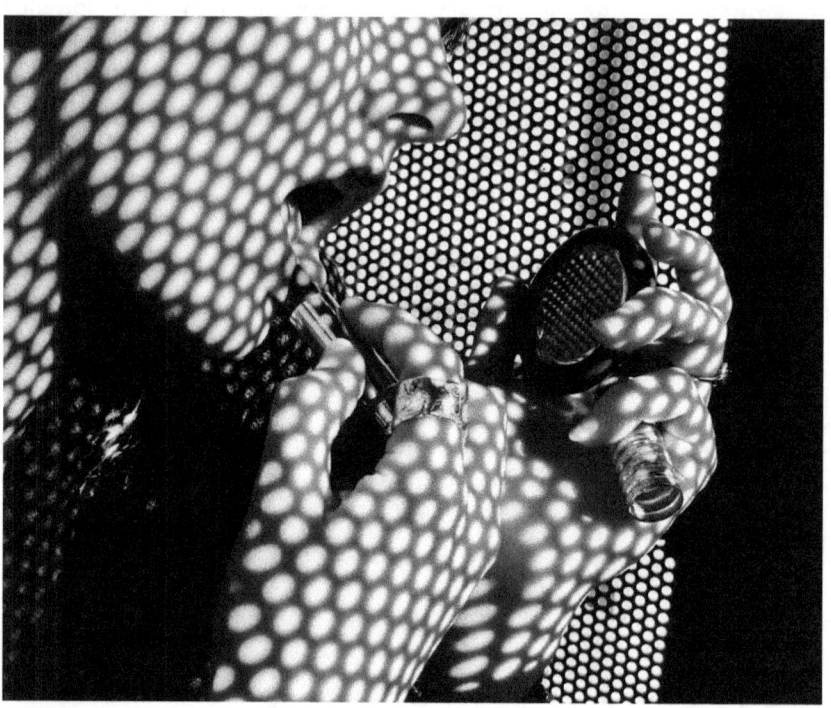

She's never going to give up. She doesn't want anyone playing her. Taking her place. *I'm still here*, she laments, tugging at a ragged edge of scarf she's dragged over an ear. *I personally prefer to play myself.*

An only girl lounging in the sand, sweeping her hand through grain, smoothing a sand castle to cradle her body; a sarcophagus, her legs gleaming in the sun, freckles rising on her knees. She'll do anything she wants to do, she's not too delicate, she'll withstand the shock of losing all her hair, ringlets caught by a boar-bristle hairbrush. Even her eyebrows have to be filled-in, absence invoked by a thin wax line.

Lying naked in bed, the covers absently falling from her clavicle, the ridge of her breastplate, her hands occupied by a pint of ice cream and a tarnished spoon. She says it isn't right. She's not talking about herself; she's talking about her mother. Mother sprawled across the twin mattress, gathering cats in her arms, flaps of skin dangling from biceps, cooing to the kitties, her feet protruding from the edge of worn sheets, toenails long and crusted with filth.

Women are supposed to be pretty, mother says.

The tendency of images to be still, matched with her will to move, one moment fixating on *thirty-six feet of sea*, the next marching like a majorette, holding a tallboy of beer aloft, pumping it in the air. Never turned off or on, always showing her teeth for the camera.

Her canvas shoes squeak all the way to the beach. *Thirty-six feet of sea,* she exclaims, covering her eyes with the flat of her hand. The irresistible fancy of her footsteps in the sand. Following her into the waves: *I'm afraid I'll get knocked over,* she laughs, and dives through a crest, surfacing on the other side, all the shore behind her.

Mother's always interfering, reaching out to bring her back: *Where are you?* Mother's voice echoing through the house, under floorboards: even the cats aid her in their pathos, cawing for her as she's running through the house, feeling downtrodden, wanting to confess, her pelt split at the seam.

The war took all the boys I danced with, she says. When will they ever come back, she wants to know.

She will give out, give up, give in to the trumpet vine, the delphinium, the hurricanes moving in to sweep the house away, ramshackle of fruit crates, the record player, empty ice-cream boxes, litters of kittens and rhinestone studded brooches. She'll go along with it all. She'll go down under Mars, leading anyone she can catch down through the moonlight, dropping, rolling, gathering dust.

TEN

She does not assert yes or no. *Why wonder?* she'd say instead, though she never says much of anything. Silence is a style she wants to develop. If she needs to, she'll stand for a long time and then slowly drift out of reach. If she shows too much enthusiasm, her fans might tire of her. She wants to go around turning heads, snagging glances like a school of small silver fish. Maybe it's difficult to attract attention from so far away. A double-spread close-up is one fateful inch too far. She despises a planned schedule and would rather admire her own sex life in tabloid magazines at the drug store checkout stand than meet the plane on time. All the thin, weightless girls waiting to retrace her movements, the red carpet beneath her flesh. Her influence is quite clear: the necessity of a penciled-in brow, kiss-proof lipstick. Her interest absorbed by post-consumer waste. If she needs to, she'll take a taxi. She'll say, *Dear,* she'll say, *Darling, where are we going? What am I doing?* In the backseat up to her arrival, and afterwards tucking in fistfuls of scotch, kicking her heels off and pushing them with bare toes beneath the driver's seat. As fast as she can, still radiant. Ladders in her pantyhose and the car in reverse, a slow and continuing process towards home. She has been to the market without being recognized. This is a correct description: basil, olive oil, one tomato. Her crumpled receipts in the parking lot, a set of items small and secretive. Solitude is inevitable for her; she can't let herself surrender. Her loneliness brings her closer to satisfaction than regret: she lights another cigarette, observes the stack of blown-out black and white photographs of boys who've loved her. A process carried out in the context of her ordinary life: boys last seen having keys made, making mysterious phone calls. Undesirable and unthinkable at any point, fictional situations she can hardly implicate herself with.

ELEVEN

She went onto the street. She saw from this place; she looked at what abounded and made no comment. The wind swept away her quilted robe and she looked very cold-bloodedly and she walked to the outskirts of the world. She did this and she was not seen; no one asked her to stop, or put a barrier in her way.

She got there first.

The road was rather long, and it was very narrow. The pavement had some holes in it and through these hollows different forms and different shapes rose from below. She went right on. Even when she was alone, she had electric lights for eyes. The places along the avenue already familiar to her, a kind of fog enclosed in glass. The same solemn, weary light falling on her. A swollen mist so close that she could attempt to embrace the air but she stopped. She stopped and she passed a cat that spoke to her. Sometimes they spoke to her and sometimes she spoke to them. It is very strange. She stood and looked at a place where she used to live and it was very overwhelming. She was no longer acquainted — a reason to start looking again. Otherwise there would be repetition and she would grow very bored, she would look at this furniture and accept the things that have been here for such a long time.

That is what makes her keep walking.

She does not really care for walking. She wanted something immediate to do, something that could happen very fast and she started then.

The house became more enclosed and more enclosed. Now it is even more enclosed. She has not walked completely around it since it has been enclosing. She cannot come out in the open any more.

The shadow she makes has several forms and she gives it form and she is always trying to outrun it. That is another reason why she does not need to travel. She doesn't like to go this far. Night and day are very necessary for walking, the sun and the moon: very important. What good is the sea without salt?

TWELVE

Sunlight sifting dust, shadows set by unseen objects strike her out. She allows that omission, encourages it. For the duration of her lifetime, she has been standing all alone on a hilltop against a crowded sky. Each cloud carefully placed to draw attention to her taut and furious face. She's often worried about something, and occasionally the worry migrates into terror. She takes whole mouthfuls of air, canceling each cloud. At this rate, she'll drift from the ground, her body's quick moisture sluiced into stars. She'll rise collected in her fear; she couldn't stop if she tried. She could start a development here, a return of light through glass. There's no point in going ahead; murder will occur, the earlier the better. She holds her hands at ten and two o'clock, the wind smoothing her hair like a man's large, calloused hand. There are strange, still moments set up against a needful urgency and speed. It may be her imagination, or she might be right; truth is tricking all around her.

THIRTEEN

A very young girl walked in unannounced, surprised to discover a duchess perched atop a ladder, the duchess' half-parted lips stuffed full of nails and a hammer in the duchess' hands. The household staff wreathed around the ladder, watching as the duchess hung a portrait squarely on the wall. *So irksome*, the duchess sighed, *they don't know what they're doing,* and climbed down, her great skirt bobbing, a tiny boat lost at sea.

A very young girl is condemned, unassisted, to supply the daily needs of her own nature if she hasn't any coins. If she found a penny on the street she might bend and pick it up, but such things are disfiguring to ladies.

Somebody might look at her and laugh, and she would rather eat a parrot cooked in pastry than give one inch of dignity.

The labors of a very young girl should be cut into convenient pieces. Thereby she may return again to the woods and bring back baskets full of pine cones. Pine cones are tolerable to the company of ladies, though sticky. If she holds a pine cone in her hand there is a chance it will bite her. She might have a feeling like pleasure. The small wound, like a pomegranate seed in her palm, gives her leisure for a sigh. She won't have to make any ornaments today. She can forget the heroes of antiquity and drift instead into torpor, her substance soon changed to a paste of talcum and cologne.

A very young girl needs an object for her petulance. She has nothing beyond the cares of her household, and she must see them done right. Everyone else is to be considered too stupid to know the difference; in this way, she wrangles for herself the governance of everything, and a right to cast away those duties indifferent to her. Deciding what to do first is a weary process that often ends in pains to preserve a velvet dress. She is expected to take this commitment. A rusty nail will keep a hydrangea blue, if she walks in and discovers the duchess has disappeared. She might climb up to the very top of the ladder, let the painting thud to the floor, and take the nail from the wall with her teeth. Much is to be said about utility.

A very young girl must soon return to her own silvery fluid. There is no difficulty in distinguishing her; she's pinned at her waist a buckle polished to the highest order of reflection, the brass still warm and ecstatic from her effort in struggling through the window. Once outside she might be permitted to wander a little, though the climate may be too intense to be long endured.

FOURTEEN

She had to run up and down. On a clear day, she could see the coastline, and on her heels a tide of water rising from the basement, a crust of salt slicked on whitewashed walls. She could hear the sound of her house rising and she really didn't want to. She'd been put in touch with a woman she'd never heard of before. *Only boys have heard of such things,* she said. She'd started to get frustrated with just waiting. She'd gone into the living room with a wax crayon in her hand and scrawled something across the wall. The shape she made was like a kind of map. She strained her arms over her head and lifted up on her toes and when she was done, she stepped back.

She kept her place. She reached forward, turning her cup in its saucer like the dial on a kitchen timer. What she'd wanted was to be easy and pleasant. By going upstairs, she has a place to be alone. In the attic is a small room with window looking out on the street. Early in the morning, she sits there looking out into the treetops, and the sky, and whatever she can find. In the yard around the topiary she'd pruned, scallops and hermit crabs and sea nettles squabble in the parched grass. This is where the flowers come through. She has to find a way of staying awake. Her house shifts and sways, buffered by the buildings around it. She loves beautiful things.

Between this house and any other house, there is a wilderness, a vast sea of light. She's learned to like what is around her. The sun high and deafening, the way to her house not long. She proceeds from the start and never thinks once of him.

Sometimes she'll stand at the top of the stairway, looking down.

Moving through each room, hoping that nothing is missing. The furniture hunched under old bed sheets, more disordered than the address proves. She lifts a cloth from a mirror; nothing could exceed her outline. A woman's beauty lies in a man's desire for her. He'd lifted his glass and taken a drink; she'd watched it move down his throat and disappear. Staring at herself, she finds she can't agree. She stares in the mirror until she blushes at her own frank gaze. He only had the appearance of knowing what he was talking about. *Damp chasms and mouths!*

The familiar assumes rightful shapes. She confides to the credenza, pulling open each drawer. Of what value is beauty in a man? The dark is all within each room.

Sounds come from within the house. The dull, persistent ache of busy machines. A little metal clashing shut, an arched doorway beckoning. In an earthquake she'd let the walls break without her.

FIFTEEN

Crumbling her face over a teaspoon, her nose wrinkled like tissue, *Achoo*! The microphone follows like a moth drawn to light, fluttering delicately over her head, its dainty wings her halo.

Holding her skinny arms out, her hands limp like baby birds, a good girl, crying for her worm.

Field flowers clutched in her hands, flower girl slowly peeling the floral wallpaper from the wall, revealing a bricked-up fireplace; no way through, no sliding down the chimney, no bats flying in the house. A bird beating itself against the bedroom window, crashing against it, not quite understanding: the trees outside so clear, automobiles perched on branches like canaries, rusted yellow, wheel wells chirping in the wind. A chandelier of wet nylon stockings hanging from the ceiling: she swings, the bottoms of her feet stained by berry juice; she's been making wine, tromping down the bushes in her bare feet.

She's always trying to keep up.

A homemade dress of sugar sacks, a pincushion shaped like a tomato; she hangs upside down, lets the blood run to her head, burn her. Wiping the oozing liquid of her nose on her mother's thin, gauzy curtains. Singing the loose ends of her hair with a cigarette lighter, braids slapping against her arched collarbones, so sapling, bent to the point. She reaches and pricks her finger on broken glass, the window shattered by the bird that beat it. Holding her dress out to make herself float, spinning in the room around her, flowers shattering on the walls, falling at her feet. A circle of salt on the floor, dust on the bedspreads, the house lounging into despair, curdling in its foundations; it's better this way, more perfect; foiling her long, white hair. Stacks of old newspapers and empty jam jars scatter sunlight, stun her. The microphone slips in, she lifts her voice so that it might hear her, *It's really real*, she says, sweeping glass with a dustpan. Lines around her eyes like gleaming desert sand swept up in ruffles by a hot, fevered wind. She stands herself in a suitcase, kneeling and folding herself, a cashmere cardigan, side by side to paisley, sequins, fox fur.

She'll catch a king in her outstretched hands, come home crowned. The microphone follows wherever she goes, a mist clinging to the molting leaves pasted on the forest floor. They wince as she stomps upon them, pumping her arms, car tires scattered like flowerpots rolling away. Things happen to her because she is ready to say *yes*, all the time no matter what. If she sees a pony standing alone on a hillside she will take him with her; the pony appears now and she takes it as it comes, pulling him by a rough, hairy rope. The pony's lanky trot rousing dust from the road. A herd of redheaded children following, shouting. She's too small to lift herself on the pony's back; she walks beside him, strutting in her sneakers. The moon under her feet, the moon diademing the pony's head; he whinnies, tossing the moon further into the sky. It bounces back, settles between his ears, perched forward. *Could you do that again*, she says, in a sudden fervor.

The pony left behind, trailing his lead in the dirt; the girl counting each drop of water plunging from the kitchen faucet. When will it ever stop? She does nothing to shut it off; she can't turn the handle tight enough. She counts one, two, three and keeps on counting.

Please wake up, she says, so frustrated by what she can't control, rising from the floor all covered in flour, the smell of plaster and a wound on her back smothered by a spider web. Washing her hands and then lifting them out of the water, her fingernails clean, not a speck of salt; a trout trafficking in her hair, the cars cradled in the trees chorusing until light leaks, sunspots.

II. FILM STUDIES

ONE

She needed a way through.

The arc of her ankle suspended in the air, an arabesque on a rhinoceros: a whimsical composition. A horse stampedes through her head, whinnies towards the wind. A soughing sound in the wind. *It's like fucking a child*, they all said.

She hasn't taken her nap today.

Equestrian latitudes, falling into shadow. Standing in tall golden grass, cinders falling from her fingertips fill an empty swimming pool. Her head haloed by mustard grass doused with sun, her lean body leaning colt like to the sea. She'll go down, she'll go up, clutching her cigarette, setting fire to the room that entraps her. She'd rather be shoplifting, eyes as big as teacups, a diva in a stretch limousine, devouring long city blocks, towering buildings. Gangling girl in a leotard swishing shoulder-grazing earrings back like hair, switch-hitting lip kisses, turning her cheek side to side.

Seasick she slew mink, ermine, fox; feasted on their flesh, pressed blood stained fingers to her eyelids, a thousand weasels staring out from her fine-toothed face. On a bare mattress floating in the middle of the floor, ship sinking, retching over the side.

Kneeling in a field of long grass, a girl surrounded by prairie, her skin like honey, camouflaged by the summer, it's already time, summertime: the crows waiting in the trees. The sun already setting. She's not allowed to play with the other children. She doesn't know what to do with herself when she's alone. An inability from which she'll never escape.

Her morning routine, an egg in a porcelain cup, one earring brushing a reedy shoulder blade, her head lopsided, somewhat ridiculous but preying on that dissonance: something awry, aesthetic incongruity. An eyebrow pencil in one hand, a cigarette in the other; she reaches again and again for the cup of coffee topped off with brandy but though she raises it to her mouth her lips never mark the edge with their print of red, a mark as distinct as a fingerprint circled mercilessly round the tip of her cigarette.

There are ways in which she's not pretending but it is difficult to see what those might be.

She wants to be taken seriously and still have fun: sliding her bracelet up and down her arm, her voice breaking over the din of conversation around her, her voice cutting all the others out, a long string of *Ohs* issuing from her lips. She'll store her best lines for later. There are things she'd rather not do. She's already looking off or away, murmuring, *Oh darling*, clutching the tablecloth with her free hand, then rising, her hand lifting suddenly to caress the enormous necklace banding her throat. A decorative gesture of annoyance. A halfhearted scowl crossing her features; she's disgruntled by the passage of time, every moment she's coerced to sit there waiting, wasting her time. Her display of impatience works beautifully: she gets what she wants; she's served, bought and sold, looked over and relied on. *What took so long?* she complains.

Maybe it isn't a real hot toddy; maybe there is nothing there, or it has gone lukewarm and that is why she never drinks. She holds the cup in her hands, warming herself, her attention skipping on the tableau of glossy flowers, silverware and glass laid out before her.

Take anything away from her: she screams.

Be quiet, the camera's here, she says. The camera's already here. *Can you give me that line again, ach-choo!* She'll react based on how she's followed, she'll let herself be convinced that she is still beautiful, *But sad*, they will say afterwards. *But sad.* Sitting on the beach, needing to be convinced of the tides' ceaseless pull.

Her frailty, calculated to seduce. She couldn't stop herself from knowing how to recognize an easy mark. She didn't mind being in the way. She wanted out. Her concern for economy: one would not be enough for her, she needed more or a way of making more: the capital of the kisses she sometimes allowed.

The trouble is in finding the right image. She wanted to make something of herself, no easy compromise on her integrity, no resignation to a formulaic girlish beauty. Crashing her Mercedes on the way to a party, cutting off her hair, dying the rest quicksilver to make herself a model, a girl going grey in her youth. She cultivated bad habits, urged men into her bed then set them on fire. She couldn't find her money; her dress had no pockets. Her pocketbook empty save for a tube of lipstick. She didn't need anyone to hide behind; she'd walk out without paying the bill. Facing herself and whoever might be watching. It's the only thing to do.

What is she trying to regain? A look of anguish crosses her, blanches her, thins her from the inside out. She'd like to dance on film, a mermaid surfacing with her hair billowing around her, her skin sheened blue by the plaster walls of the swimming pool. Blown up photographs taped to the walls, a host of disembodied faces keeping their eyes out for her. *Do you like, do you like, do you?* She wants to know, raising her hands to her breasts, enlarged by silicone injections, her own eyes orbiting far-off planets. She'll only make it halfway through, then leave or perhaps fall over, her whole body collapsing, rippling as volts of electricity shiver along her skin. She is callously left face-down; I stand back to survey the wreckage.

She is markedly absent. Tennis shoes hang by their laces from telephone wires but there is no sign of her.

There are girls in black leotards and fishnet stockings walking down to the beach with black eyeliner smudged around their sockets. They will scissor-kick sharks with their legs and wrestle each other down into the sand, sink slowly as the cliffs close around them, frat boys hurling empty beer cans from the bluffs, white stucco houses facing out towards the sea. Looking out on oil platforms, looking out on islands, looking out for her walking her dog, her hair uncontrollably long, drained of all color.

What has been taken away is already lost. The space in front of a camera, which holds her steady, resolved to commit the same mistakes, to take the queues she missed the first time. In order to compensate for her losses she grins so that her whole face is transformed into a mockery of a grin. Nothing is left of her but that smile; where she was there remains only her phantom, reaching out across the frame.

TWO

Her big, made-up face. She turns towards herself, surprised to face herself in profile. Her face forward laughs, *I can't stand it*, her earrings wind chimes thumping against bone. She's yawning, pretty teeth tombstones cluttered in her mouth.

I don't have anything to say, she says. I hear what she says when I'm ready for it. The sound moves between her two mouths, distracted by her erratically switching face, turning on and off. She drags from her cigarette, then her hand falls away, brought down by the smoke billowing from her fist. The cigarette burns, unaccommodated by what can be seen; she lights another, holds it, twisting the stalk between her fingers.

She talks toward someone off screen, eyebrows gathering on her brow as she pulls a face, showing her dimples for whoever is there, observing her sprawl. Behind her, a TV set on which she stars, her face in portrait on the TV screen. On the television, she's calmer, less spastic; I can't bring to the two sides together cleanly — her whole face isn't available. Before the TV set, she mocks herself, *Can you believe it*, clearly troubled by what she's saying on the alternate sound track.

At times, the two images turn towards one another; two girls silhouetted in stark black and white. She comments on what she says on TV and then drifts, disrupting silence with frantic, absurd looks — until the face she can't see from where she sits, herself projected on TV, dissimulates and splits apart, snow banking the screen. Then gathering back to flesh, lips heart-shaped, a worn-out beauty mark on her cheek.

She doesn't need to say anything to keep the camera on.

The camera draws back so slowly, her earrings swing shut. She says, *Oh me?* Someone inserts their arm from the right of the screen and turns the dial on the TV set, interrupting her. The sound pitches, rolls under water; I can't make out what she's saying, clapping her hands together and giggling. Covering her mouth with her hand, smoke flowering around her face: carnations.

She tears open a package of gum, chews, tossing the wrapper to the floor. Her cigarette drawling her mouth, the gum stuffed into one cheek. Her short, clean hair and the enormous cocktail ring on one finger. She has something to do. *It isn't really, it really isn't,* she says.

The arm reaches in, turns the TV off. Her face in profile shrinks to a tiny white box and then blanks out.

No — don't! she says, loudly, clearly.

Gesturing to herself, *Me?* she's amused. The screen behind her flickers —
she's back on, images of her face sliding down a ladder, toppling over each
other and finally registering in place.

You can learn everything from looking, she says.

Somewhere in the distance, a telephone rings: the sound of the receiver
crashing into the cradle so loud she starts. Her face in profile on the
television behind her whispers into her ear. And nothing else. *It's so much
like every other day that I spend,* she says.

How can I think about clothes? Her figure on television speaks dreamily, a
steady monologue only halted by the disembodied hand that interferes.
From this angle, her face radiant, feline. Facing forward — almost grotesque,
crossing her eyes, thrusting her tongue against the bent-back ridge of her
teeth.

*You can't go out anywhere without beauty. It just can't be done. I wish it were
simple.* She can keep going. If she weren't doing this, what would she be
doing? Sailing in a glass bottom boat, driving a little car, only room for her
and her fur coat. *I can't do that,* she says. *Do people really do things like this?*
She closes her eyes, both at once. The channel on the TV changes; men in
cowboy hats stride across a flat landscape, then the signal goes out.

THREE

Her white arms sweep his tanned, broad back.

Her breath takes a plunge, he moves to cover her, his palm gliding against her hip.

The recognizable, overwhelming drone of a plane engine disturbing a cavalcade of clouds.

She crosses her arms over herself.

He takes off his pants.

Oh I'm so cold, she says, *the desert,* grey and blue. She makes a light with her face, all around her mounting rock and sand, a steady burning darkness. *Maybe we should put it off until tomorrow.*

If I don't do it tonight I'll never do it, she says, their two nude bodies, thin and absurd — a layer of fat would have saved them from shivering like this, but they keep going. Her hands move, seeking out a soft, hot place to rest, *I've got you.*

Time lapses, lags. She's tangled in dust and dirt, a film of grime over her flesh. Tall mountains brace a saturated sky, men approaching on horseback.

A heartbeat bangs against the screen. Boys in red kerchiefs and ten gallon hats, authentic cowboys in leather jackets lined with lambswool. *You turn me off completely,* she says. Boys perched on horses like figurines, a line of horses tied to hitching posts, cowboys discussing their hairstyles, heads down in the wind. Leather fringe, lassoed hat bands.

She whips him with her crop, startling the horse, *Ha! Phony!* Slapping him across the face with one leather glove. He takes her, kisses her; she falls back into the mud, laughing.

She gathers herself and makes a run past the camera.

A fierce cold light rising out of the sand, bald rocks. Bouquets of nopales, silver buttons and turquoise. *I want to ride a horse.* Freckles and bruised lips. *I want you to be a part of us* — he counts the names of men. A belt circling a tree branch, buckle swinging. *Listen honey,* he says. Queens in suede and pearls, eating beans out of tin cans. Three shirtless, breathless men, stacked chest-to-chest, bare but for their pointed, heeled boots. The wind overwhelms all other sound, knocks against a man crouched on a low-slung fence railing, propped up on his rifle. *I've had too much exposure to this outdoor life,* he says. *Men carrying on,* caught by their desire.

She strides on her horse, lashes down: *Get off my ranch.* Faces of men, worn and sleepy, eye whites rolling.

In the sun she's clean. They tear her from her seat and strip her shirt off; she's laughing but trying to cry, she's required to cry but laughing. They jump upon her, rub dirt into her flesh, pull her hair; one holds her legs split, shouts, *Get in there!*

She sits up suddenly, pulling her clothes to cover herself, *Oh my hair, look they've pulled my hair out.* Her teeth chatter, her clothes clumped around her. *One more impertinence out of you and the fuck is off,* she says. *I've been humiliated!*

He takes his hat off, forces back a lock of hair. *All you've done is take off my clothes,* she says. *Let me kiss you, get your mouth down here, put your tongue back in and stop digging with your fingernails,* she says.

He leaves her laying beneath a tree, away from the sun. Her roughed face, cloud of red hair, the embryonic curl of her fingers folding into her palm.

FOUR

At the edge, waves break. Sand rolls out, spreads. Sand surging to fill an expanse. Bright crests of sand, and his blonde hair, combed back, furrowed tracks carved by aluminum teeth. Water sifts bits of seashells, dried bone, tendrils of hair and weed. He shines, the sunlight flatters him, casts his skin flat and bright.

He has a knife he scratches himself with, a switchblade held behind his back. His hand does the work of reducing driftwood to a toothpick. It doesn't matter what he's here for, only that he looks so right. Through binoculars or otherwise, he knows he's being watched – he does everything so slowly, unnaturally. His successful beauty, a gleaming cocarde of sand coiled around him.

You must understand discipline, he says. She recoils, laughs, lifts herself slightly out of her seat better to see the boy swept in from the sea. She wants a little revenge. She only wants to make him suffer. She only wants the taste of salt-drenched skin.

You try too hard, he says. His confidence is hard to catch; he offers it, withdraws. He's worried she'll take off all her clothes, laugh at him.

A trick of the light, an oasis; a boy's broad back split, a blade of hair.

The accidental happenings they're waiting for will happen and will not be accidents. The camera comes between them: a way of getting nearer to each other without actually touching.

Waiting to take his place before the mirror, where he rightly belongs.

The way he keeps filing his nails, he may really be worried. He can't stop, he keeps going; he may continue until he grinds his fingers down to the palm. *Not the past, the present*, he says, refusing to return. He wants to start from here, a boy born beautifully from the sea, lying in the sand. An image of a man alone, lit by a solid expanse.

When she goes down to him, there's nothing but broken glass and razor blades.

Her dreadful ability struggling against mounting waves. She might scream, use that as an excuse to grab him.

FIVE

Her face barely here, eroded so that only a palimpsest of her features remains: her hairline, the sweep of lashes, the impression of a mouth. Chalk marks only the camera can see, the scar between her eyebrows receding. A face that's been pressed onto celluloid like a flower between the pages of a book: whoever she is, eluded and out of focus, a light streaming steadily becoming increasingly brighter, washing her out. The camera has made a decision to leave her this way, a girl haunted by herself.

Fuck you, she says.

The camera draws back slowly, she's sitting up in bed, dialing a number on a rotary phone, the wheel spinning and clicking. It's late afternoon and she's risen, woken by the sunlight peering indelicately through her window.

The camera follows her and the screen goes blank, absorbed by a patch of sticky black, the telephone receiver abandoned on the bedspread, dial tone. She returns to the phone, lifts it, mumbling something about pills — she's unsteady, still between day and dream; the camera came and caught her before she was ready to begin. A plane passes overhead, the familiar sound of its engine unsettling clouds; she holds the telephone to her face, makes simple requests.

I'd like to see her better but no position I take renders her clearly. She remains blurred, a figure sucked of clarity, an apparition billowing puffs of smoke. She's never without her cigarette; even as she stretches on the bed, lifting her legs perpendicular to her body, she's smoking, or the cigarette is smoldering in the ashtray, waiting to be pressed between her lips. When the camera comes too near she moves out of its way, drops the phone, *Shit!* she says. She puts a record on and sits down at the vanity to do her makeup. She puts this and that onto her face and meanwhile the telephone is ringing, the cord trundling from her mouth like a long, twisted tongue. She flips the record over, her small body swallowed by a blot, an ink spot.

There's something awful about her routine, her efforts to shake sleep from her body, to get herself motivated to start a day that's already leaving. All these things she's done before, and over again. She's a strange, thin insect doing weird, secret things in a small hole under the earth. She doesn't stand or sit straight, her whole body tends to fold in on itself; her impulse is to subside, but once she begins to sit still and say nothing the camera comes to love her and cannot stop. She lies back on her bed, calisthenics or shaving her legs, everything too distorted to be either or all at once.

One, two, three. Now I see her here, her torso creased in the middle like a greeting card, her black underwear, her black tights. The beauty mark on one cheek, the scar between her brows that mimes a unibrow, the dark eye-makeup wedded to her eyes. This girl is sharp, definitely here or there, ready to be anywhere. She lights a long pipe, sends smoke whistling and says, *Are you going to wake up?* She has only one earring on.

A thousand stairs, I walked forever, she says.

I have so much junk, she says. *What am I going to do about it?*

She answers the telephone's insistent, *Who?* curling her lips up over her teeth, her neat white teeth.

He calls her and she ignores him. *I have to go and shoot a few scenes,* she says to whoever is on the phone with her. He calls her. She crinkles her face, leans into the vanity to dust on blush. Her meerschaum holding court among eye shadow and talcum powder. She sucks in her stomach, holds it. *What am I going to do?* she says. The shadow of her one earring flutters against her collarbone, rising and receding. She licks her teeth, her tongue withdrawing into its cave.

You eat a lot and you never get fat, a man's off-screen voice remarks. Her mouth is dry, chalky. She puts on more lipstick without even glancing towards the mirror. She puts it on before the camera. The camera draws back far enough to reveal the clutter of her room, a sweet mess of dirty underwear, rolled up nylons, empty perfume bottles, beads, bills and candy wrappers. The man is there somewhere but outside the space the screen allows.

You look different, he says, *but no different than you did yesterday.*

The camera inches along her body. *I have to eat everything at once, otherwise I can't eat,* she says.

GLAMOROUS FREAK

On the back of her neck there are fine, downy hairs.

She puts a dress on; *Don't you have it on backwards,* he says.

Oh, no, I can't wear it, she says. *Do I have to get dressed right now?*

She isn't ready. The blackness that absorbs and deletes her emanates from her closet. She goes inside and comes back out, *That black thing. I don't feel like trying on clothes, why do I have to try on clothes,* she says.

She's wearing only underwear, stockings, a leopard-print belt.

You might catch a cold, he says. She puts on a leopard fur coat. The most beautiful coat, she calls it; she might be ready now, encased in fur, panting.

The camera plunges frantically in and out, hitting a mark in the center of her body, a frenzied, uncontrollable zoom that comes on suddenly, seizing her.

Does this go? she says.

SIX

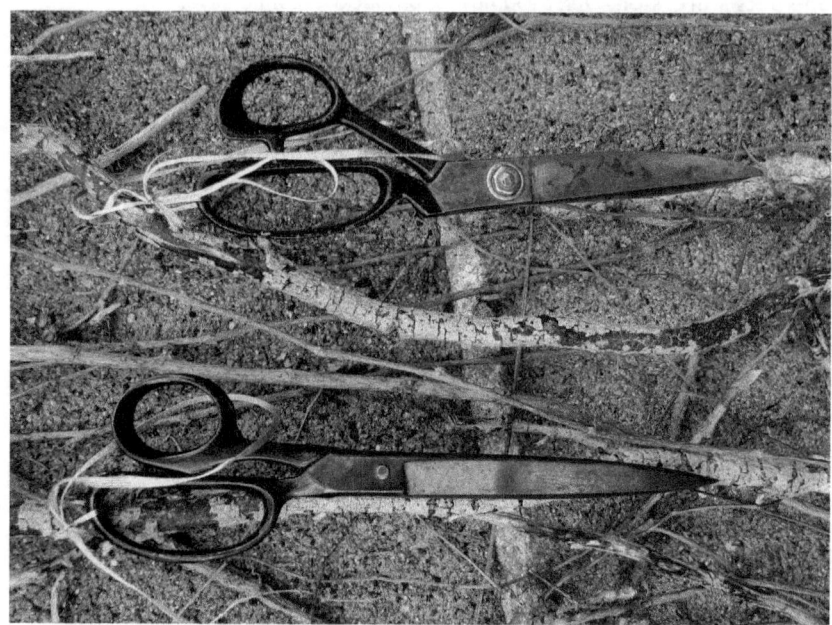

The sound of water splashing into a basin, water unseen but rising through a faucet; water filling a space outside the range of her softly furred face, light and clean. The girl holds a mirror in one hand, her scissors in the other; she brings the mirror closer to her face, as if she's nearsighted, ever-so close, attempting to focus directly on the length of hair above her eyes. When she turns her head her hair swings into the foreground, a field of brilliance conducted with light. From her face, there's a withdrawal, revealing a man in a striped sailor's shirt washing dishes – she's sitting in front of an oven, a young boy falling into her arms.

The man is washing a silver teapot, the child whispering and the girl, who might be the boy's mother, blonde and sure, grasps a tortoiseshell-backed brush in one hand, her mirror and scissors in the other. She trims the bangs above her eyes, clipped hairs caught in the vessel of her lashes. She'll make everything even; what has been divided will end aligned – her eyes crossed over the gap.

Drawers open and slam shut, the sound of furniture dragged across a waxed floor. She props herself up on the counter, beats her heels against a lower cupboard. The man ceases to wash the teapot; *Do two yeses mean no,* he says, *I forget. Usually I ask a question because I want to know* – he snaps his fingers – *I get an answer.*

Once the screen splits, I lose my place. There's an incredible ruckus, a competition between two films: where to look. The girl will always be cutting her hair, an impossible endeavor she doesn't complete. If she were actually cutting her hair, she'd have no hair at all. She makes only the allusion of snipping at her hair; nothing much is taken away. She opens and closes the metal blades perversely above her eyes, cutting but not cutting, a figurative cut, which brings her face to close-up.

The sound bounds back and forth, starts and stops. *I'm not sweating, you are,* a woman says on the left of the screen's split. On the right, the girl cuts her hair, her polished white kitchen, the child and the man beside her wearing identical vertically striped shirts. Two women now side by side, caught in distinct spaces, separated by a chasm of black space but located on the same screen. On the right the woman sits on a couch, a couch pushed back-to-back with another couch, a man seated opposite her. They are lit by one light, the room they are in otherwise dark; the woman wears a pair of sunglasses, her hair cropped boyishly short.

On the left, she takes a sip of water, brushes something off her fingertips.

On the right, she crushes a wad of paper towels. *I don't want to reform you,* the man says to her. *You're very spoiled.* The woman replies, *You make my father look young.*

Any arrangement is possible here – there's an order that can be interrupted, flipped inside out. The film may start with the woman cutting her hair, or the image of a man over whose body a cold, blue light is cast. Time ascends around a curve, reels playing in succession like runners in a relay race. Brightness is subdued by distance; sound is handed back and forth. My eyes move uneasily from polka dots on the girl's necktie to the mother in drag who berates her handsome son, *Does she know what you are like, really?*

She may be silenced, or she may be allowed to speak. There are iterations in which her lips move without issue.

Undoing with her mouth the belt which holds his bathrobe closed – the belt hanging from her lips like a long lolling tongue, wrapped around his waist. I'm drawn to look away; I have no way to choose which side to watch and no disposition to favor one over the other. I slip easily back and forth between the two films: *I'd be bored in hell*, a girl declares on the right. On the left, a woman grimaces in anticipation, slams a hypodermic needle into her thigh through her jeans. Exchanges done and undone. The film on the right ends as the one on the left continues, the woman exclaiming *My dear! Come back here.* Incidents that don't hold, at least not for very long.

On the right, a boy with his hands tied behind his back lays across a bed loaded by another man and two girls, two girls dangling neckties from their fists. One of them slips the tie through the belt loops of her jeans and then reaches forward, pulling the boy's underpants down, exposing his bare ass. *I'm going to change my clothes*, the woman on the right says. There is no opportunity to maintain a center, I'm always directed away, then jerked back by some absurd thing: a girl in a patterned bodysuit stuffed beneath a desk, her long legs protruding, exposing her legs buckling on a bed, so many bodies on the bed on the edge of falling. Girls slapping each other, squealing, arms bent back. *Everything you do is so perfect, go fix your hair, get up and walk across to the mirror.*

A struggle to focus: occasionally there are defined bodies; others remain blurred. Halfway through a deliberate, carefully established transposition occurs: in one frame, there is a close up of a girl's face, another girl behind her sitting in the window; on the right, a close-up of the girl's face who sits in the window on the left, the face in close-up on the left now sitting in the window. What does this suggest? A diametrical opposition of girls, switching places, sharing lipstick, trying on each other's clothes. A voice whines, *I won't do it again.* Now the same girl in close-up side by side with herself, an instant that slips away as soon as it emerges. The shadow of a cigarette drooping from her fingers makes a stain against her face. The middle holds and hinges on this image, six hours split here and flipped over, the two sides meeting at a deliberate limit, teetering on the edge and realigning in time. What has been and continues to be an irresolvable disruption connects in a way that can't be torn.

The camera revolves around the room, seeking a slot to slip in. The walls are so thin. I hear her inhale from over here. *She thinks she can speak to those beyond – I wonder if she can speak to herself.*

That's what I said, that's what I meant, she says. The room is filled with the sounds of traffic in the city beyond the screen. A man leans his head back, hair sweeping across his shoulder blades. I see as much as the camera can see, or what it is willing to expose – the insolence of a camera that looks away from the space in which action takes place, which zooms in instead on a woman's inaudible lips. The withdrawal of the lens is a kind of slap, an ache.

I have a temptation to call her or to be reminded but the moment I begin to recognize relationships between right and left the reel ends or the sound switches sides. The way she touches and organizes herself within the film is enhanced or embroidered truth – every time she makes a demand something is retained, a build-up that allows me to recognize her, again and again, without fixing her in place. She lives in repetition.

The violence of her outbursts is unsustainable – the blonde cries out that she wants to go home.

Resolving to a single image at last, the houselights lift.

Seven

Tiers of fabric gather around her. On the bedspread her body lights, illuminated from the marrow out. She gleams precisely: not a romantic light but a clinical light, a cold light that fades her face, despite efforts to fill herself in with mascara, lipstick. An absence of color done by hand. Smoke rises incessantly from her parted lips; she says nothing, lights her cigarette, ashes on the mattress. The arrangement of her legs all angles.

Who do you belong to? she says.

A sleek black hound crouches next to the bed. The slender leash attached to its neck leans a dark shadow to the hand of a boy who reclines against the headboard, totally passive and beautifully blank.

Her earrings swing crazily from the bright lobes of her ears but make no sound. The ice in her cocktail glass reminds her; she takes one earring off. There is no code, only a girl wearing one earring laid out in bed, talking to a man I can't see. Is there something she wants? She points, her hands erratically busy, moving towards her mouth and away, lifting and setting. The boy on the bed with her arranges pillows around her back, makes a throne: she settles, the bones of her hips rise through lacy black underwear.

Is horse real to you?

I'm confronted by her profile engraved against the headboard, the plaster wall. When she turns towards the camera, she turns towards me, her face panning out: wariness captures me then vanishes once she turns to speak to the man I can't see, a man who brutalizes her, a man at whom she laughs.

She pours vodka on the Doberman like cologne. The boy in bed with her scents her as well, rubbing alcohol into her narrow joints. *I can't help sweating*, she says.

Taxis blaring in the city outside her small apartment.

Lights her own cigarette, spills her cocktail on the bedspread. The boy rests his cold glass on her flat stomach, caresses her long legs, her legs that are almost all of her. *I hate pretty*, she says.

Shadows hover over the bones of her body, find no place to rest. Her bones gleam, could pierce the boy cleanly. She runs her toes along the dog's leather leash; laughs. The sound of a siren in the street and the boy leans and presses against her, kisses her so that her arms rise mechanically around his back and clasp.

The man who watches and taunts her is barely there; his voice acts upon her so she can't resist. She'd rather reply than kiss the boy she squeezes. *I'm not vain, I'm self-involved*, she says, defending her beauty. She crushes herself against the boy, buries herself: meanwhile the man sits in his armchair, reading aloud to them, a narrative they can't follow, their tongues running together. She draws both men to her, her attention sliding back and forth between them, holding them. She hooks, sinks the boy into her bed. What is he really there for? A promise is never given; kissing is enough, or all that is desired. She sits up, sighs, reapplies her makeup, checking her compact, her body propped up against the boy's body. She combs her hair, readies herself for the camera as the camera records her movements.

She looks at the boy. *You've looked at him long enough*, the man says. *Don't push him away.*

SHUT UP, she cries, *what are you doing here?*

She is derailed, by what she can't say.

She interviews a new beauty, a boyish beauty that could replace or replicate her.

She can't really ever be present as long as she's being watched. The kiss given for the camera will always be a kiss separated from the functions of the mouth.

The encounter begins with caresses and kisses. The unreproductive remains of her kisses: the boy lying on the bed. The man keeps saying, *You can do better than that, come on*: he wants a money shot, something to see. She lingers; I don't see that she is doing anything wrong: she's clean and sharp-witted, ruthless towards herself. She is certain she's criticized. She throws her cocktail glass off screen, aims for his head, misses. Her room full of empty bottles, perfume bottles, vodka bottles, the bottles that held the pills she took.

The boy curls and slithers about her, her body doubled over him. Her efforts to assert herself often fail: she's either drawn to pleasure, or her hackles rise. Her repeated attempts to change the subject remain neglected: there's another agenda at work, an insinuation that she needs treatment, buffered by the pillows arranged around her, the way her body is at rest. On the bed her passions are acted upon, the man who accuses her of coldness sitting there watching as she tries to pull the boy, the boy who replaces him as her beauty. The exchanges between them are movements done without the faculty of feeling. *Truth and publicity are the same to you*, she says.

She takes his place on the bed: who is beauty for, who will wear beauty, claim and keep it? Her silver hair, the silver hair of the cameraman, leaning into the viewfinder, watching her frolic on the bed, gestures he's seen before. When the film runs out she's still talking, a violation of the reel. What happens when the machine turns off, when the man who released the button comes forward, when she gets off the bed and exits, when the boy lies there, primed, and the man off screen to the left dissects the lines of the frame.

EIGHT

I'm impelled to keep looking. Over time, I empty out. There is very little evidence that he's alive, that this isn't a photograph. No indication of what holds me here, but I'm holding and I won't look away: there's no confrontation in his gaze, only time passing ticked by batting, beating. I look on, continue to look, unruffled; when he smiles I'm struck, startled by the least absurd twitch.

Her mouth droops half-open, the gate of her teeth clang shut.

She smokes as a way to pass time. Three minutes is a long time to sit so still. Her face must itch. She aggressively diverts her gaze away: stares resolutely at the floor, shyly swivels her eyes to the side. She can't settle with any certainty. Her brow furrows, her tongue flops lazily in the trough of her mouth.

I can see his eyes roll through his dark sunglasses. His lips are very pale, drained of blood. His own glowering shadow rises up on the wall, dwarfs him. I want to see before the reflection on his sunglasses but only see beyond, his eyes languidly half-closed.

Her gaze is so direct, specifically for me.

Thick, weighted eyelashes droop and roll. She wants to say something but can't. The beauty of her silver, glossy. She sees herself reflected and satisfied. Smiles broadly, fades to white.

A man's blunt jaw lit from beneath. He's composed, angular. A shadow cleaves his face, uneasily even. He swallows, shades of black and grey gather and collapse at this throat, a hard knot unbinding.

She wants a fight. The camera has invaded her. The camera is inarticulate in the face of her anger. A lock of hair falls forward from the crown of her head, sweeps a black shadow over one eye. She thrusts the offending lock back, a scowl settling in. Indifferent to whatever happens. Wearily erased.

He doesn't quite see what the camera is doing: he has other things to consider. A face with eyes omitted. Pulling off his personality: cigarette smoke rises.

At first, he is above himself as well as below. The frame fixed. He undoes his necktie, prepares to relax. Lifts his collar up, a scraping of nails on skin, mute. He has a part, he slick. He puts his tie back on, knots it, folds down the collar, looks forward.

Looks that come off the screen, looking in between screen and space.

His head revolves, spinning or spun. He doesn't fall over but I'm dizzy, watching him whirl. He's only a head turning in a dark room. A head turning by itself. Bodiless heads, lined against the wall. I could exchange these heads with my own, unscrew my neck from the base. Every face turned towards me is my own face looking back. No difference but indifference. A distance a finger width gone too far.

A woman lifting her hair up around her: this long. Her arms extend above her head, puckered elbows turned in. Her hair will carry her. Long, snarling black hairs, a girl caught in a tangle on tape. She stuffs her long hair into her mouth, chokes, spits it out.

She laughs too much. Makes a kissy face, blows.

This is his good side. His mother cut his hair, nicked his earlobe with silver shears. He gulps, his lips plump. The surface of his face is distracting, scarred. From here, he's too close but so far away. The pores on his nose, every detail, down to the tears he hasn't cried. Not close enough to be abstract and unassailable, to be loved. A face I can't love; a face I can be a fan of.

She looks right here. She looks shampooed. Her heart-shaped, her almond. She avoids the look of the camera and therefore avoids me. I'm lonely without her, this room dark, filled with purring.

Long-range shot: close: closer. Back and away by degrees, backing up. Moving in to cut. He looks, feels how fat his tongue becomes, lying quiet within his jaws. Worries about what to do with his hands, hands smoothing down the fabric that lies against his skin. He sits and waits to be told what to do. For this to be over. He pitches. His look is for me. Faces barely lit, features rubbed out, white out and black in. A face I can dispose of, forget. What is the difference between these barely moving, waiting heads and headshots, body bags? Cords of men and women, all in grey, arrayed in white.

Nine

Boys surround her like potted plants, cutlery and crocks in a plain, white kitchen.

She's simultaneously vulnerable and captivating, her leotard, her opaque black tights, black high heels. She thrusts her legs out before her body, follows behind.

She sneezes to gain time, to think of what to say. When she begins to speak, it will be the first sound. She opens her mouth but the kitchen appliances work against her, drown her out. The refrigerator, the blender, every kind of machine running at once. Her face washed out; she perches on a stool, courted at the kitchen table. A man sits opposite her, shirtless and hunched over. A photographer walks by and takes her portrait: his flash stings, sends the kitchen reeling. There are moments where she vanishes, slips in and out easily, clutching her cigarette. While smoking, she sneezes, she needs a line. A whisper reaches out and catches her, tells her what she'll say.

Holding a slice of coffee cake in her bare hand, her hand white like a porcelain plate, her fingers snapped together. Licking her fingers clean.

She's like a chorus girl in that leotard: she might start dancing at any moment. The kitchen crowded with bodies, all huddled around the table: a girl snapping gum, smiling and laughing, filing her nails.

She lights the pilot.

All of a sudden, she's down on the kitchen table, a man's hands laid about her neck, a collar of flesh and bone.

As she leans her head over the edge of the Formica table, the photographer enters, takes a picture. She lies still until they tickle her.

She's often laughing.

She sits up, says, *I burnt my hand*, the table wobbling under her. She spreads butter on the burn she gave herself. She shows her hand, the table holds her place; they move around her murmuring sweetly.

She's too big to stay here forever.

She sneezes, a breath held unwinding through her throat. She could actually be sick: her sneezes border between polite ah-choos and violent, whole body shudders. She names out everything in the room, counting the china and silverware. The kitchen empty, her affectless voice attaining a rearrangement of objects by number. She enters alone clutching her makeup bag. She begins to do her face, sneezes, takes a tissue and wipes her face off. The face she wears is a face that she puts on. Her sling-back heels rest on the seat of the chair next to her stool, her legs raised, her two knees like little birds chirping on a limb. She places her mirror on top of her knees, sweeps a mascara brush through her lashes, her face pushing out against the light, her eyes pitch black. While she does her makeup, a man does the dishes. Water sloshes in a coffee cup, the photographer enters, takes a picture. She holds her mirror and a man enters, kisses the back of her neck. A plane passes overhead. She leans into her mirror, her back curved like a spoon. She fumbles in her bag for something; a clatter of makeup brushes, blush. Plates clang in the sink. What is left once everything is removed: a girl holding an empty bag with her face on.

She drops everything, makes a racket. *Darling*, she says. Swings off her stool onto the tabletop, her hips thrust up, up, her legs peddling the air.

He kisses along the length of her calve, his dishwater hands laid flat on the table, the water in the sink left running.

She powders her face, sneezes into her compact, a flurry.

He always wants to strangle her. There are wires taped to the floor and walls that prevent him from his succumbing to his motivations.

She wants to put her makeup on.

She removes her necklace. *I don't have anything to wear*, she says.

She takes off her high-heeled shoes and washes them with dish soap and a sponge in the sink. She hands her soaped shoes to a man and he dries them with a dishrag. All along, she has been dropping her ashes on his bare chest.

TEN

Have you ever seen this woman before? Not like the others, calling out for time. A position according to daylight: a place she wants to take.

I hate to be touched. She asks to be touched by letting herself go; she pleads to be let go once the scene is over, but there is a sense that the camera will never stop rolling.

He turns in profile from left to right. He lifts, spots, rests his hands on tight thighs. She lights her cigarette, sips from a paper cup, her body in a little black dress thin and flat like a Popsicle stick. She splits the cigarette, shares, inhaling a long while before letting go. She struggles to fill space with the noise of smoke, the men around her ripping the pages out of books, ripping and tearing as they read, crumpled sheets gathering on the floor.

A man in a houndstooth suit sits with his legs gaping as the boy is taken, undressed. As a man bridges a heavy chain between his gathered fingers, she knocks over her cocktail, her eyes widening too wide, eyes popping and POW the salary man leans back even farther, laughs as the men drip hot wax onto the boy in the background. A pretty tea light, dappling and singeing his skin.

She smiles pleasantly. Her arms wave and snap around her body, hands flapping and rocking like a waterwheel; she moves against the light, chases it away so that it hovers above her, radiating her face. She is placed here and out of place, only recently added: all the real things happen around her, the script running, lines read. She says nothing, keeps herself busy and out of the way, folding her legs up on a steamer trunk, her feet dangling so they can't brush the ground, the portion of the screen directly opposite her inhabited by a twirling disco ball. By doing nothing, she calls the camera to her: whatever is happening is less interesting to see because she is here, extraterrestrially arrived.

The men behind her shave the neck of the boy with a switchblade, an eerie chalky scratch that can't be heard, a static of the knife rubbing against his spine. They twist his arm behind his back, hold him keenly, spit in his eye. A cigarette is lit and awarded him.

She lights another cigarette, lights a candle; a man takes the candle from her and slowly tilts it over the lean chest of the boy, his other hand reaching up to clamp the boy's squirming face, covering it as with a handkerchief, his thumbnails two cold quarters on the boy's eyes.

He's slapped, the splendid snap of his flesh springing against leather.

Leather has a shine.

Black tape wrinkling on his chest like a dead snake lying in the sun.

What is she looking at now? She crosses her arms over her knees, gathers herself up, leans her forehead down to her knees, wilts a little once she's arranged herself. Her long earrings swing, scythe her jaw.

The boy is crying, spitting blood. They punch him but it's a playful punch, performed: his heads takes the hit, jerks back but slowly, too slow. The gentle flick of leather belt against his backside only alludes to a real violence that could be done. There is no wound or puncture but the figure of the girl who is bored of all of this. She punctures, punctuates these pretty, interchangeable boys.

ELEVEN

A chapel of horns chuckling, a thick velvet curtain of blonde swathed across her forehead. Long black lashes, two millipedes hinged above her cheeks. Her hair held back with a rubber band taken from round a newspaper that morning, swept into a knot while coffee boiled on the stove. Her face closing in, blurring until it rises on the surface of the screen like the moon reflected on water: even her most visible features fade.

This is how to disappear on film. Rolling back her face with a quick snap to the whole band gathered around, a child sitting at her feet, a tambourine in her hands like an embroidery hoop. She perches on a stack of amplifiers, her little boy in cowboy boots, a striped shirt, buttons pinned to his chest.

The camera moves up and down between them, then to the wall behind her head, making quick zooms into her face then out again, her hand inserting a beat rattle banging against her tambourine. A resonant curdling, the long neck of a man's guitar stretched across his lap, the scooped neck of his black T-shirt. Recovering what shapes there are, the bow on a violin moving in a suggestive way – suggestive of a worm finding it's way out of the earth, reeling in the sun. A shadow pulsing on his jaw. So many ways for the camera to come in between them, to take the opportunity to strike them out in black and white, the sound they make a sort of pitch and moan, bent elbows and pulse dissonant with the camera's tracking.

Stops and starts, rises and falls, lured out and back in again in a mechanical, precise way; not a bodily thrust, a mechanical movement, from here to there exactly each time, whipping out a measuring tape. Wallowing in the dregs of her faded dressing gown, distracted by the clucking and squabbling around her. Whatever the camera is doing she pays no attention to, her glance straying to the boy, a child with his mouth open like a baby bird.

The camera swings furiously back and forth, agitated; the camera taking her image and shake, shake, shaking her wildly, so she trembles yet is still, totally still, tangled like any other girl beating her tambourine. A static, droning noise, carried out and reproduced; all the men wear dark sunglasses, glistening opaque eyes, a buzz snaring sound, whipping back into a squeal. The little boy shakes a rattle in one hand, his mouth slightly ajar, tongue laying at the crux of his teeth, the camera zooming in and out and into his mouth, thrusting into the gaps in his teeth, into a space in which he isn't, an empty silent space beyond everything that's going on. And up and out again to a man using his fingernails as guitar picks. Reeling around the room, swooning with the droning music, caught up in some frenzy. Swaying and rolling, as if it had a body itself. Shadows lengthening under her eyes, a colorless blush rising on each cheek, as she smiles, casting everything away.

A luminous head of white blonde, hot blonde, a parallel between her bright head and the round tambourine in her hands: an orbit of two molten planets. And the camera nodding itself side to side. How long can a little boy sit there in his cowboy boots shaking a rattle? He stands and walks to his mother, clutching her legs in stripes, their two striped bodies clashing, horizontal with vertical. The drummer's sunglasses slide down his nose, his eyes peek out over the top, flicker. And cut.

He's moving out of the way, picking up his rattle again, exhibiting a painful look, biting his lower lip, the camera dividing him and his mother, stuttering on her face, her quick smiles, her frantic hands playing a guitar with a butter knife. He doesn't quite look sad any more, if he ever did, if anything other than what can be shown; a boy sitting next to his mother and the camera's movements against him, of which he's had no experience. An arrangement of men around them like a court, his mother's blonde hair for a crown. The camera's lights off and on, the room gradually shot to black and then released. Locating blackness in other ways: black towers cast by the drum set, a solid stripe on a man's shirt. Small flecks of light interfere, increase.

Lights full up, they carry on as before. A slow, steady beat, a soothing rocking, a little boy sitting in a guitar case, as if storm could come and carry him away, floating through the city in his makeshift ship. The music stops, she stands with one hand lifted slightly away from her face, a slat shadow across her eyes; walks off screen. They all stand and walk off screen, leaving an empty space of stools and amplifiers and microphones. The dull noise of machines plugged in but not on. A desperate uselessness in solitary stools and amplifiers and microphones.

They come back on, stand and pose for the camera, one man holding a camera, raising it, depressing the button. Outside the set, an inky dark where they've been for so long, a shine of silver paper, and men in suspenders. A darkness that fills out everything, makes a charge. Wires leaking across the floor, men standing around with their hands on their hips, unoccupied now by guitars or drumsticks, and one man with his hand curved around the alphabet. A cord. There's film left, it runs until it runs out, capturing everything that happens afterwards, after the film is already over, after they're done. She kisses him cheek to cheek. Abruptly and purposefully: she's ready to go, her purse slung over her shoulder, gloves flopping over an extended wrist.

TWELVE

She's given a name before she begins. When she begins, she is before, already smiling; her eyes catch and drag the camera so that the film stutters. Her eyes move up and down as she's followed; the increment of her pupils' traffic in the socket makes a map to get lost by. Unsure of what's beyond or what she might be looking at. Her mouth lilts, lips spreading wide, wider, her small teeth like the tines of a plastic fork snagging on a continuous stream of sentences, erupting uncontrollably from somewhere deep in her body. A viscous plaque of letters accumulated beyond the proscenium of her jaw.

I want to become a nun, she says. Nuns walking through cold corridors, black dresses all stuck together, the static shock of several women clumped into one. She's nude, folding her arms over herself. No habit to cloak herself in beyond the continuous issue of her lips. She isn't sure, what next? She holds a stack of menus and fans herself, her body peeping through each flutter.

The zip of the film rewinding cuts her.

Her eyes can't be missed, settling into her face like two black spiders, crouching. Her hair is lifted; she rubs her arms. Dressed in makeup and little else. She pins, loops; she might be repeating things she's said before, in other circumstances. A voice off screen *Hmms* and *Yeses*, edging her on. She doesn't need much, only the camera rolling, an audience. She has a lot to say and keeps saying it. A few words are enough to last her a long, long time.

If I didn't say anything we'd be in the fallen leaves, she says. Her mouth widens, lips coming apart then snapping stickily back together. To take up the cavity between her tongue and the roof of her mouth she says, *Jump!* spreading her arms wide, her body suddenly clear, a woman stranded behind a diner counter, coffee cups on a shelf behind her turned upside down so they won't collect dust.

The camera draws back; at the counter, two semi-nude men in g-strings perch on stools, another man situated at a table in the foreground. She folds her arms back around herself, her fingertips resting on collarbones. She's grey, a bloodlessly silver narwhal, all the men around her stuffed into pink, piglet flesh, frothed with curly black hair.

Would you like to hear some more? she says.

She walks around the counter holding the menu before her drawling hips. *Will you imitate a bird for me?* she says to one of the men, and he closes his swollen eyes, ringed like coffee cup stains and smoothly draws air between his teeth. She lights a cigarette and looks at him: he's half-asleep already and she's barely started. His face is falling, collapsing as she watches, his eyes running like eggs. The rest of him so absurdly thin, he might be a bird; a stork, with long legs upon which flesh clings too tightly, pulled taut. He sits at the counter and she stands behind, and behind her a man in the kitchen, visible through a rectangular window.

At first, I imagine the rectangle behind her is a mirror, and that the chest reflected belongs to the man with his back turned to the camera, the gaunt man, but his chest is smooth, hairless and trembling. In the room beyond the woman at the counter, a man with a bared chest does something, not listening to her. Beyond even him there is a clock on the wall from which a black cord hangs a comma.

She does most of the work of speaking, she's working here, she's supposed to be the waitress, serving time, bringing out prepared stories, voices she's done before, practiced gestures. A boy with flowers sprouting from his spine crouches next to the stork and she reaches out to him, rifling her fingers through his hair.

He reaches out and pinches her nipple.

Miss, he says.

She slaps his hand away, *Stop pinching me, I do have a name you know — my name…!* She keeps the counter between them but asks him to keep jumping back and forth over the barrier, *I like to see your bottom like that,* she says.

All around her, leather booths and sugar in neat white packets, salt and pepper shakers, place mats, pewter cups of cream and chrome counters. As a boy begins to babble, she complains from her counter, cuts him.

She moves out from her station and sits at a table in the foreground, flinging her cigarette. She continues to hold the menu before her, facing the men at the table across from her, but her side is exposed to the camera's position, the soft angle of her breast rising, her arm lifted and resting on the tabletop. The camera pivots on her face, starts and stops. *I told her I gave myself a new name*, she says — she can say it better by not saying much, only to keep saying, say something say anything, to keep talking until the film runs out and she's left with nothing else to say. Her nudity second-place to her conversation, the drill of her voice relocating any interest away from her body, which sits dumbly at the table in its lipstick and mascara.

He's so shy, he's afraid to be touched, she says, and the man with painfully knobby knees leans away from her.

But I have possibilities, he says.

The shadow of her hand upon which a cigarette is perched, straining its long neck, suspended over the man's bare chest.

She moves forward to tap out her cigarette; her features blur then snap back, settling into place: her mouth, the beauty mark below her inflamed eye.

In what movie, he says, and the camera cuts, collapses them and sets them back up again. They're always starting over but starting from a new place, not repeating but keeping on.

She reads out the available options, resting her chin in her palm, whispering to him, *Hash browns, beef…*

Whatever you got, he says as she leans in closer to him, *Is that what you want?* A ridiculous innuendo, leaning in mouth to mouth, their two mouths near touching.

If you don't lean a little forward I'll fall off the chair, she says, putting her arm around him, *A little ketchup,* her lips smacking on his skin, her grey hand on his ruddy neck, *What am I going to do in the meantime?* she says, her arms flopping around his shoulder. She says, *You cut off your beard and mustache — why?*

She's coming close, traffic passing. They sit together at the table kissing, done with ordering food, she prints her lipstick traces on his face, licks his lips with her tongue squirming against his teeth, The bones in her neck aching, and leaning over, laughing into her lap. *Ha ha ha,* she says, *I think I'll quit.*

Holding a compact, running her finger along the line of her lips, tracing a path. *I've found something better to do,* she says. In the small mirror cupped in her palm, she watches herself making her face up. The men sit around her, nobody ordering anything, although they've been drinking and licking their lips and suckling and sweating steadily. *I always did look like I'd just got out of bed,* she says, *because I had just gotten out of bed.*

The stories she tells go here and there, she could be saying something other than what she is saying but this is what she says, either to fill space or because it is important to her. Even if no one were listening, she would still be whispering. Her eyes quite wide, *I couldn't stop giggling,* she says. *Finally I couldn't stop. Finally, I decided I'd had enough of it. They kept calling me.* The man behind her with the smudged eyes presses his fingers against his mouth, sighs. Her eyes rise into her skull, looking for her cue.

I would've liked to go, it was awfully hot, all those gold fishponds...

She stops and pauses, looks carefully off screen, a sound of a door closing somewhere beyond what can be seen; *Are we still running?* she asks.

She'll keep going as long as she has to. At some point, she might stop but she isn't sure how or when; she might have to come up against something. Tumble or trip.

She'll outlast the film, as long as she is being recorded she has the stamina to continue a conversation she's not committed to but one which she will strive to carry on as long as the film lasts, as long as she can launch herself forward, her mouth moving a chronicle along.

So much time left to fill: I'm ready for it to end before the end; the man next to her rubs his eyes, looks utterly frustrated and bored, a strange, cruel torture to keep them on camera when they've already given all they've got – the impetus to linger they must bend to and obey.

All I could do was look.

Or maybe she is worried she won't finish her story before the film runs out, she's moving faster and faster, trying to cram it all in as long as the spotlight is upon her – but she strays too long over a cool glass of water for this to be true, she repeats too many things, she concentrates on her expressions, shifting and turning, the gloss on her lips, her teeth wetly shining.

So uh getting bored, she says.

No uh I like to listen to parts of conversations, he says.

But it's really more of a monologue.

Somebody mumbling you get just as much, he says.

Can we turn it off for a minute? she asks somebody, whoever is there behind the camera, the cameraman, the strobe
cut
flares

GLAMOROUS FREAK

Right in the middle of making love, she says, lights her cigarette with a match. *I read a lot of trash.*

A ticker tape, sentences all strung and hinged together sputtering from her sharp pointed teeth, her pink glossy mouth. One continuous stream, bouncing and tripping as her attention wanes and wavers but coming back again and again.

I thought I was frigid, you know I would have tried anything.

Snorting smoke out through her nostrils.

Start it again and I said stop
I can't do it
One night as I was… she says and the film blacks out.

THIRTEEN

The discord of her plumed, plump lips magnified beyond proportion. A position expanding on her salt encrusted eyelashes, a forehead festooned with curls. Her lips pausing, pushing out a breath, smoke receding. A man in a woman's guise flossing her teeth, furling her mouth wide. Give her the face she wants, the face she needs: a face she can change, put on. What does she need beauty for? She is occupied, only susceptible to innocence.

She springs up from the operating table, sings *Ave Maria* just to show she isn't a floozie. The camera pans beyond her, climbing up to the ceiling and all the way around. She says, *Ravishing, ravishing.* The camera trawls, the spotlight empty; she wavers on the line. *If I can't be in movies I guess I'll go out shopping*, she says. The camera settles on her, a dead weight on the broad, angular lines of her jaw.

She's in the light and out, selected. *I'm someone, more or less beautiful*, she says. Her thin fingers lifting a skinny tie from a boy's chest. She unzips her dress and lets it down, the fabric wrinkled and rolled about her torso like a sock.

A light lurching, staggering as the camera moves to capture it. The zoom, fervent to find her in a satin dress, leather elbow length gloves and a rubber bathing cap.

The sun setting on her boulevard. She's still the star, gripping the handle of her purse, an arrangement of bridegrooms around her in a hemicycle. Her stubble showing, lipstick leaking from her lips. Today she is all woman, her purse packed with hand gloves and marriage certificates.

After an interrogation, she pulls her satin dress over her head, her arms rippling with muscle, green grocer's fruit.

FOURTEEN

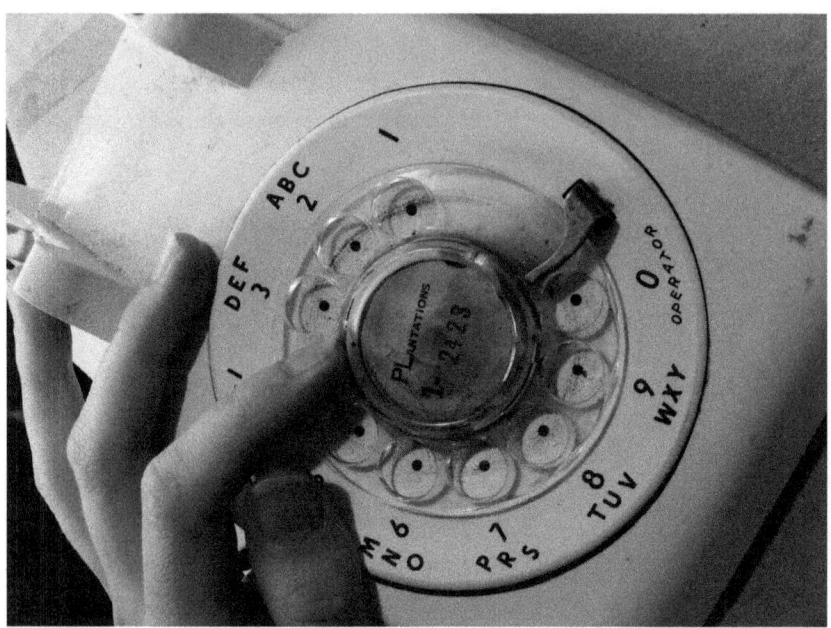

She feels for a heartbeat, her face pressed up against the flat pane of his chest. Between his lips he sucks a lock of her hair. *Take off your clothes,* he says, and again, *Take off your clothes.* He lifts the bottom of her dress, inching it over her thighs, but she pushes him away. *Take off your clothes,* and she takes a ring off her finger, tossing it carelessly to the floor.

Mary, she says, and he replies, *Don't call me Mary, Mary.* So much is said, sudden language filling the depression left by past silence. Certain things they say skip and stutter on the soundtrack, burbled words collapsing on the tongue.

She stands up, circles around the couch. *Had I known I wasn't wanted!* she says.

A zipping forward onto his bare throat. There are hesitancies, cuts caught on the stack of cards split in his hands: the close-up shuddering to a stop on her face,

a girl with glistening lips, freshly wet. *I believe everything I make up*, she says to him. She does the math, undoes her buttons one by one. Each movement has a cost, a consequence. Her bared breasts make a closed parenthesis filled by two hyphens (she's put bandages over her nipples). Her arms crossed over her chest like a pharaoh in his tomb. *There's a few extra bones,* she says, lifts her head.

I don't even like being touched by you, he says. They lie on a quilted bedspread together; she is propped up on her side. *I find you highly repugnant,* she says and drags the bandage off her breast, throws it on the floor.

A new dress, she says, *a new new dress*, a frantic strobe splices, she folds her legs

over him. Perched at the bottom of a ladder, clutching a stuffed doggy, she leaps up and lowers herself to straddle his waist. *I don't want you to be anything*, he says, *you can be nothing.*

A colorful mouth might spell English, but *Love, love, love*, she declares. To make up for missing moments she'll slow down, stop now and go. A tiny praying mantis moves along his lifeline, his head

thrusts

against the mirror hung over the headboard. A boy hovers next to the bed holding a mechanical parrot – when he pulls the string the parrot says

That door is closed for a reason. The two men on the bed lock hands with their elbows touching the surface of the fitted sheet. They get off the bed and push the frame aside.

FIFTEEN

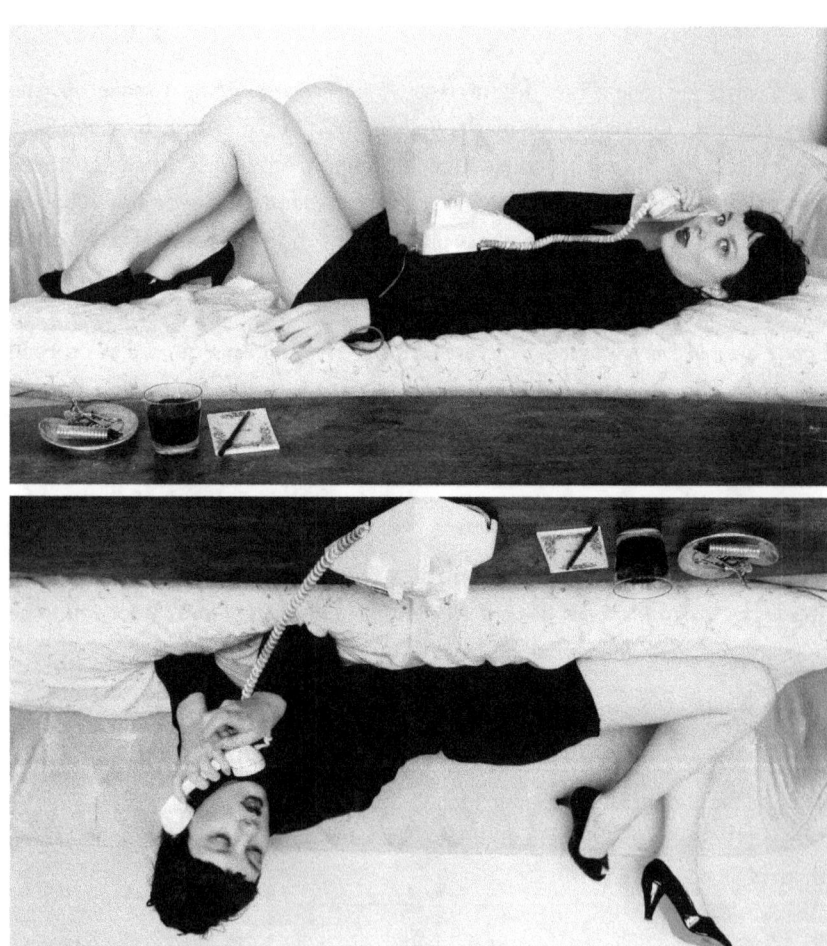

You've got to go, get up, be clear. A shot forward and through the foot of a bed, two bodies laid up, only now awakening. *Get out,* she says, but he's drifting, snagged by sleep, the sheets still sticking to his skin.

A flick of a switch like rapid gunfire, on and off, off and on, seconds faltering shy of a minute.

He brings her beneath the bed, where they won't be seen. Their feet poke out like in a cartoon, their bodies too big to be hidden. *My parents are going to come home soon*, she whispers. They settle in the dust, sneeze on each other's face. They rise from the bedroom floor like bed sheet ghosts, dust gleaming in their hair.

She puts the water on, they share a cigarette. *Before I split*, he says, inhaling.

Pulling his pants up and down.

Doing and undoing the buckle on his leather belt.

Headlights traversing black space, side by side. On a bridge yawning over a highway, in front of a chain link fence, they caress each other, topless. *Don't you have anything new to say?* One curl on her forehead mimes the sound of passing traffic, the ocean caught in a seashell. *I don't think I do love you, baby*, he says.

She pushes her foot against his face, her toes in his nostrils. Two shot glasses on the coffee table. Her legs bent like bendy straws. She knocks her knees together and

he goes through her address book, all the names aligning.

He dresses her as a queen at the kitchen table, a terrycloth towel for a robe and a hairbrush for her scepter, all red and gold. The packaging of a queen, the girl inside obliterated by the camera's passivity. She lies across the tabletop, *Don't you dare my dear*, she says, *I'm moving.*

He says, *Don't stop, don't move yet*, and she sits up.

Tough.

Once her name has been removed, it is hard to know who she is. I record what happens; I cannot call her. Her body has never been found, she is declared. She rocks back on her heels, refuses him. Behind the door she won't open, there is only a solid wall.

His hands pass over her face, skip and jump against the features that eject outward: her nose, her pursed lips. She's never made love to a bullfighter. The circuit of his hand over her body: he leans in to kiss her like drinking from the sink, gulping at her lips; she extends her long, strangling tongue.

Sixteen

Do I have to speak louder than this, louder? Can you hear me? she says.

You couldn't possibly hear this, could you baby? he says.

Can you really hear this, really? She laughs, shakes her hands, long earrings frothing, puckered silk and rosary beads. Eight seven six she blows smoke from pursed lips four twelve two one *What?!* she says. Bodies cluttered on the screen — *Who is in it?* she says. So many bodies that some bodies tend to disappear, into mirrors and back alleys, almost completely naked, it takes so long to say each name of every person here.

She calls each name, *My dear*, the camera panning to find a face to land on: is this her, could this be her or who is; this is a glass table top reflecting a bunch of flowers in a vase. This is love on the dressing table, a girl dropping hairpins and blowing a kiss, clutching a cup, reading a story from a magazine. *I can't say I've been doing much.* A necktie a bowtie a cigarette, a microphone they pass among them; she clutches at her rosary and pauses. To make up for lost time. White briefs; dreadful fur; a cuff folded back over an elbow; a flex of her knee. Creeping hairs on his belly caterpillar, clinch up his chest. The sound of motors revving in the street. *All you hear is this and that.* Her and this and that. *Now that she's dead, you never hear anything about her, this or that.* Bodies cluttered, dirty dishes.

Tomato juice in paper cups, he pushes the microphone away, saying *I hate that thing.* She's suckling her cigarette, her rosary in her free hand, seated on a stool next to herself in a mirror, at the wrong angle. Trying to remember her prayers, who she might mention, all those acknowledgments. Never sweet enough, to pick and preserve each name. Hiding all her secrets in the accounting, letter by letter and line by line.

The vagrant image of her tender, downy hair flipping up on the back of neck; her thin, ostrich arms. Another girl lying on the floor, dragging on a cigarette, settled beside a mirrored disco ball lost from orbit. She takes a roll of paper towels and starts tearing off a sheet, giving it up. *You realize what it's costing you*, she says. Very serious, her big earrings so ridiculous, *Jesus me beads* in falsetto, then deep, then again.

Give it to me, she says. The girl beside her with a bow tied at her neck, so that she'll remember. *Let's think of fun*, she says, dipping her fingers into tomato juice, flicking red specks at his white dress shirt, his jean jacket. *Can I say something?* she says, *You have ketchup on your face, anything for a little color.*

As they progress they gather more, more and more has been recorded, and what is it: everything that has been going on, and continues as long as the camera is turned on. *You've made a mess, you naughty boy, go in the corner and hide,* undoing each button on his shirt; peeling it back, he lifts his arms for her. Several people are partially undressed, or overdressed: her rosary, her earrings. An awful clutter of stuff and bodies all clinging together; a guitar on a coffee table next to a girl spread on the ground. She's lying with her back against a furniture dolly, perfectly formed. Somebody's wounded, something's happening. Something they can all sing along to. *I can't give her the right answers,* he says.

Opening an umbrella, rolling her wrists. Her earrings fluttering, like they might take off, reel round the room, sip from each cup: but sutured to her ears, pierced through the flesh, extended into her. A boy wears a plastic bag as a stole, and the effect succeeds as fur cannot. *I think it looks rather stylish,* she says. *I just don't know what to do,* licking her lips, turning to herself. *I don't know who to undress next.*

She looks at herself in the mirror but the woman who is speaking isn't her, it's not her voice. Her mouth moves but it's like the tracking is off: not always her I can hear, a wreckage of voices colliding. *Find out what she's saying,* he says. *Is she protesting?* A spread, a stage, stop upstaging: take a gander. Everyone takes a paper napkin, folds it neatly in their laps, once, twice. *I should go and wash the dishes. I want to do my hair. I am doing it.* Pressing her hands together, going through the motions but not really doing anything, drawing a cross through her chest and amen, of the holy.

Try again and, *Oh dear,* she says, putting one hand to her head, *Oh dear,* she says, *bless!!* Her earrings won't stop. *Play with us,* she says, now and he says, *Now,* and she says, *How I am supposed to know? And when?*

Louder! he says and she shouts *Death!* and he says *I'm afraid you can't be heard.* Clutching herself with her arms folded, then hands together, the camera zooming in from the crowd onto her, only her, her raw cheekbone and the earring out of control.

You better be thankful, she says. *My dear, my lovely. Go bother somebody else, I don't want to hear about it.*

That will do, he says.

Covering her ears with her hands. *Hallelujah!* he says. She sings along, counting along on her fingers, who is real and who is faking, *Hallelujah!* and stops, and stops singing. He turns to the camera, *What's it all mean?* She stops his hand, pushes him out of the frame.

Let's play pretend. I can't be intellectual, there's not enough time. I can't come in. Collapsing on each other, laughing and human flesh and a laughing girl who put out the light and, *Oh, and, How dare you!* and cigarettes lofted high, ashes scattering, *Oh here I am I have been can I…*

SEVENTEEN

Occasionally a blip within the camera covers a lapse, an instant machinery came too close, saw clearly and then masked itself by switching positions, moving away. On the soundtrack, there's a noise like a sizzle and a pop, a timer unwinding, an attempt to insert these too-intimate details, which could also be details of no certain consequence: what is private is so plain and unprepared for glamour.

Through a red filter, a red halogen light staining every inch of film, he bathes. Water pours from the showerhead, red-tinged water loping along his back; he takes some pleasure in the heat of the water moving over him, soap lathered on his face. The film hiccups, moves closer and backs away.

From farther away more is exposed but the camera never moves too far from the warmth of his body, boldly lit. Around his neck, he wears a ring on a chain. Whose ring is it; whose hand reaches out to turn the camera on and off, creating these disturbances, ellipses between which he

smiles

dries himself off. A close-up of his lips, crooked teeth: his lips voluptuous, pursed like a duck's bill. His wet hair clumps together and he combs it back, smoothing locks flat to his skull with one hand – he should be looking at the mirror outside the screen to his left but instead his looks into the camera, combing his hair, a glance to the side where he can take a real look at himself. When he's ready he stops, poses, stoically looking forward, his eyes distracted, a light flooding and casting him out.

EIGHTEEN

My body rejects this kiss, spits it off. The animal absurdity of two faces too close together. They blur, the edges baffle, break off. This so close kiss, too near. Her hair thrown back, his mustache sealed against her face. His mouth moves over her, takes her in: suckling the shell of her chin, skin pulled taut. The woman wears a wedding ring, but is the man kissing her husband? Is this an illicit kiss? If I am a witness, will I be called? Will I testify how long a kiss can take, how many takes of a kiss? Two mouths neatly bruised, lips and tongues like battering rams. Wedged together, his mouth overtaking her face, his tongue reaching for a hook: he'd crawl right up inside her, disappear. She'd wipe her mouth on the back of her hand, burp.

Two bare-chested boys in tight, belted jeans embrace. The image of each other. Two boys grappling on a velvet couch, smooth and slim, the pause of velvet. Deduced by the radiance of boys. Two ordinary boys, suddenly beautiful on film.

A woman with lifted wings drifting over her eyelids kisses an old man. Her manicured nails sink into the pulp of his cheek. She sits on the left and he sits on the right: the kiss is given from right to left. He bends to kiss. To receive a kiss is to be positioned on the left side. To be shorter, smaller? Her head is lowered, comes up against his shoulder. I like tall men. He pecks delicately at her, nibbles, she laughs and smiles, breaking away to check him.

Everyone is kissing each other. I watch; I am not kissed. I'm reminded of kissing although I'm not sure what I look like when I'm kissed. The kisses on the screen are unreal kisses, too long, drawn out; I've never seen people kiss like this. A spatially uninterrupted view. A kiss that lasts so long gives me nowhere safe to look. The woman falls in the light, the man lowering to kiss her mouth in shadow. A tongue moves sluggishly in and out of her mouth. They kiss without reservation but also without haste: smacking and switching positions. The same girl kisses a different man. She's traversed to the right side of the screen, taken the dominant position: he accepts her kiss. A kiss could be drawing blood. They kiss and are not alive, but steadily and surely moving. What has been sealed, a pledge or pact? Faces fit together like landscape. Vulnerable to each other, eyes closed, intent on pleasure, pausing for space. A gap where their faces meet expands, fades to white. Now a man who kissed a man kisses a woman. Her face beneath her eye, her mouth. The face is open to any sort of kiss: the lips speak to the flesh; nothing is said. The kiss is unreadable.

NINETEEN

I have been watching carefully, too carefully. The cat has fallen asleep, overwhelmed by irreconcilable structures. It lies prone with its front paws stretched out so longingly in front of it. The cat utterly indifferent to the voices tickling the tips of its hairs. The lap of the woman on which the cat rests itself, passive, suffused with warmth. The woman looks disarmingly at the camera – her gaze is split down the middle, she stares and stares, willing herself away. Only the cat has truly abandoned itself, sprawled in her lap, a white lump. The woman must work to sit so still, to prevent the cat from bounding off-screen. The woman herself is very appealing; there is a beauty mark on her breast, above the neckline of her dress. She cradles the cat, she positions herself like so, just so, like this. She is restless. Above her splendid figure two men stare with equal disaffection; the track their eyes follow crosses back and forth over the woman's head. The cat wakes and cleans itself delicately, swiping its wet paw over its face again and again. The woman is not disturbed; the men look on.

I may have missed the point. I keep waiting for something to happen but nothing happens. The starlet writhing in the foreground draws up her legs, rubs her silk-encased calves together; she clearly gleams. Can there be a bruise? *That's good*, a voice declares, muffled and reverberating outside the screen. The voice I can't quite hear has an effect on the four people arranged around the couch. They are listening, intent and very still. My own shadow passes over. I collapse against the wall, embarrassed and out of place. I am making too much noise. I'm going to have to pay for this. I can't transform the distance between their look and mine into a palpable event in time. Too much has passed. Once the camera has fixed these figures, they are already dead, moving so silently here, jerking in their flesh. If unattended, they will all turn black. The woman, caught in the unremarkable act of only sitting still, takes no notice of my discomfort. A heel clicks and echoes inside but outside the space I can see. The man leaning above the couch smokes and then tosses his cigarette away. He kisses the blonde without breathing; their faces lock together, no visible sign of relief or ordinary pleasure, only two mute bodies caught in the rise of one movement. I'm terrified and I want to leave. I can't leave until the credits; will the credits ever come, the lights turn on. What I have missed carries weight, worries me. A cat, languid, camps in the woman's lap. A clean white cat, difficult to fix.

TWENTY

Oh, I could be a darling. I could nearly see through, I could be silently offering platters of hors d'oeuvres, transparent gelatin and cocktails. I could be dressed in furs. I could be beastly, I could tear apart the living, drip fat from filed teeth. The leavings of my incisors in a faceted jar on the windowsill.

If he's still looking, I'll disappear. Into the tunnel, a small slight figure receding into the darkness. At the last moment, I'll shake my ass. I'll shake my ass as I wash the dishes. Once I pass through the hillside. I'm all swallowed up, in the belly; I'm underground. I'm buried. I'm coming back. I have so many things that must be done. Nothing would bring me back but those things that can't be left unfinished. I could've been a mistress, I may have been very remarkable. I'd an opportunity and I'd been very clean, I'd changed. I'd kept myself. I'd gone though the options available to me and projected beyond what I could immediately obtain. It's hard to say where I'm going. At the bottom of the hill, I could emerge into any sort of situation. The people surging toward me may be on the way towards their own preoccupations or they may want something that I have, they may sprawl me from my high heels, I may tumble from the heights of patent leather. I may lick. I could be suddenly touched; I could shine. Things happen when I make a movement. When I make a movement, I am deliberate and I want something to happen. Anything could happen. I'm always looking for connections, walking up and down crosshatched escalators, switchbacking, threading and unthreading. Somehow, I will wear my dress down, I will make it very clear: not exactly. Not quite precisely. I have very little to declare but so much to suggest. How does he know I have taken my last few breaths?

Lifting my chin and gazing upwards, OH. The whirl and click of the machinery that observes everything I do, the system I have set in place. I am often watching myself. I am watching myself and I am silent, concentrating on my own pleasure. The simple act of breathing provides so much relief but to go through the process takes so much attention and exhausts me. I look forward and then I look away. I think of which side is my good side; my face is not perfectly symmetrical, from a spot-on view there is something disconcerting and not quite right. I tilt my head backward, my throat offered, a long white track, the bones arching, pulsing, my mouth barely open, oh and oh, a motion I keep repeating. Is it pleasure or? The mouth that moves against me, the mouth below. Moving without stopping, the ceaseless procession suddenly too much I Oh, lean my head back, crown grazing the wall behind me. White washed bricks, and the hair on my head swept behind the fetal curls of my ears. There is something simple, infant about the expression on my face, I'm not sure what it is. Watching myself doing this. The collar of my leather jacket thrusting against the split ends of my hair. Hanging and brushing against, rocking back on my heels, back and.

Oh. Wiping my mouth on the back of my hand, the print of my mouth on my hand, a red smear, my hand reaching up and clenching the air, attaining nothing. But I cry Oh and I cover my face. I have no shame. I don't smile, I draw my lips back over my teeth; there's something disaffected, something taking too long. I crush my eyes like grapes, two black pits overshadowed by the fringe sweeping across my brow. I'm all glued together, creased at the corners, crying out and holding on, prolong this action, the act of standing here while. Something is against me, I am held, fraught and filled with darkness, my tongue a black lozenge slipping down my throat. Nostrils flaring like two commas. Bridged by this suckling sweetly, lifting and falling and oh. And don't stop. And there and then. How long can it go on, what is it possible to endure, a winding tight and furrowed. Falling forward into the light and suddenly. Simply tail, leading out.

III. How To Make A Mermaid Tail So You Can Wear It Around The House

ONE

I am grateful for the resistance offered by a line pulled taut. Something like the white T-shirt disturbed by a girl's small breasts. I hadn't anticipated facing the multitude. It is fiction which offers a problem of selection – I could turn, I might recognize a part of myself here, or a narrative point of view. My urge makes it necessary to distort by imagining: if I call up a surge, I feel it in my own body and I'm falling forward onto the sand, saltwater soaking into thin cotton. Rolling waves released for an instant, then falling back. If I imagine I am weightless then I am underwater, even though I sit so still. Where to insert a period, a paragraph, or a page? From endless grooming and reapplication of lipstick, words are extracted. I draw my hair off my shoulders and clasps it in one tight fist. These motions might translate my desire or limit it. A continuous reversal is at play: I'm influenced by the machine I work on. I shift space: the machine requires so little of me only commonly accepted movements, two hands together serving to facilitate and push. If I continued I would crash; I will crash, I am crashing. I might show a small blemish or make the mistake of spilling. The solution for a flaw is to make the flaw a part of beauty. I don't want anything to happen that I can't control but success depends on accidents. Accidents that perform an operation, offer a resistance to vision: I leap at the thrill of being recognized, called upon. I never wanted to be shapeless but I won't tolerate my name being mentioned, I'll wait to be determined by surrounding space: the air lifting and emptied out. As long as I continue, I can keep going. If I can focus, I'll be able to recognize the flickering hurricane knocking tree limbs against the door, figures cutting through the rain. A glimpse of force that will flower. By wearing the clothes of other women, I will allow myself to become haunted, and learn to make a sacrifice. Once I allow others to speak, they go on and on and on, a sudden release of language; small pieces of meaning, rejected and discarded, littering the floor. I prefer to shut them up, pull a long strand of hair off the woman's coat as a way of silencing her. A stormy night and in the hallway umbrellas clot their leavings on the concrete floor. Those who have not yet spoken are deceptively present, full of menace, but I shift, delete, and fill my tea. The danger of being alone is that I continue to refer always to myself and then my frequent and repetitive glance from the keyboard to the screen which takes in nothing but extends itself. At first, I see what can be used. I assert a specific sound, a long, drawn sigh. As earlier as later, I seek to cultivate a personal record, a confection of girls tempered by weather.

As long as I can keep watching, I won't miss anything. Whatever I miss, I'll be unable to duplicate. Any interruption will spoil, the surface will collapse; there's nothing to buffer unanticipated burdens. The door holds up the wall around it, the room beyond closed with cardboard, dotted lines suggesting furniture.

She wants to be taken out, left on the cutting room floor, swept up.

What is really happening here if she isn't even coming close. Objects engulf and overwhelm: the mirror she holds and turns against, the omnipresent cigarette drooping in her hand. An armor of meaning around a mirror, difficult to penetrate. The mirror could be a coffee cup, a toothbrush. The effect of not finding satisfaction in the object's ability to resonate: I want to break it, look behind the curtain on which the film is cast. The meaning isn't there but here, where I am. I have to talk about myself; if I eliminate my eye, what will be seen?

The bounds made between female bodies so haphazard as to be inconsequential. She appears again and again, divorced from herself.

A delight in unreasonableness, inconstant gravity. I swing from left to right. Stripes vertical or horizontal tell me nothing. She struggles to seize a position of dominance, though the films are so often working around/through her, pitching against her. If her position were a more familiar one, like riding a bicycle, she'd be steady.

Things I've been doing from the beginning: giving and taking away, an unrelenting repetition.

Films force me to go further than I want to go: to keep watching or get up and leave, which I have done. Even when she teases him, she's posing, demure. What's risked is tightly controlled, specific; she might say anything and he reply; the camera will coolly observe them. There's limited manipulation on the part of the machine, in-camera editing fixed definitely at the turn from on to off.

I want her to play me in a movie of my life. If she wants to be beautiful, she'll become beautiful. She is beautiful because she speaks directly to the camera: between herself and her image on screen there's an act of faith.

It comes across. When color is introduced, she blooms: there's nothing more astonishing. She's playing me in a movie and she wants to do it her way. I want to be revealed in a movie of my life. I'll be replaced by her in this different version. In the movie things happen, direct experience is replaced by drama. Otherwise, I'm sitting at home watching reality television. She's enough like me, but better. The luxury of what she can do.

The difference between who she was and who she became on screen. The aesthetic beauty of her face in close-up is difficult to reason away, difficult to emulate. When the camera moves close I understand that even from here I can't read her at all. Can't find a way to finally reveal everything there is to know.

Two

There's something left-handed about the way I'm watched.

A frank representation of a stare that turns out to be charming. Quite charming. I can get at it in detail and by degrees, an accumulation of silly incidentals that often interest me. Otherwise a fascination with a barrel of stones left by the window. A wine barrel split in two, not an easy thing to accomplish. A severed leg and a barrel of stones left by the window to throw at the dogs in the street who howl in the night. While I'm steady, paying proper attention to cleanliness. A bashfulness about things that can be done in the body: *Oh, you're so nasty, so nasty!* A cat pulling tenderly at a bone.

With a cocked revolver held at my forehead, she reads me her poems.

She has a high estimation of this humiliation; she makes a lot of pretty noise. *How do you take your sugar?* She's going ahead — everything depends on this dress. I must forfeit something; I'm sound, sitting slumped; I suffer bad posture and interminable dreams of love. I'd cross out everything where I wasn't going anywhere, a memorandum made at sea, a rough, careless many or not enough.

The light doesn't directly fall but multiplies over time. I've wasted several days observing this ascent, peculiar in places and then gone forever. A sustainable increase would be a preservation from every wrong thing. I've no interest in what really happens, or in doing well. I'd rather be incorrect, and carry a stain on my skirt.

I depend for every blessing on a pale yellow rotary phone. An AM/FM radio and a manual typewriter. All things I am now attempting to dispose of through the mail. The sadness of returning two year's worth of library books. Returning to an hourly wage, infinitely repeating in space and time, edging out the homespun sensuality of sleeping in. The enjoyments of a fading world moving on this great deep.

A longing for domestic associations, a selfish love of ease. Waiting all afternoon for a thunderstorm that clips along, stuttering out a few revised drops of rain. The sun in departing beauty over wavering clouds. There are few moments of pleasure and each one will be made and asserted. Where shade rests, I stay solid, carrying a cup of salt.

THREE

Anything could happen in the next moment; I'll stand in the shower, on camera and off the water will continue to pour without ceasing, ceaselessly setting up the situation: I have to stop stalling. No matter what I do, what dress or new hat I put on, to the camera I look like me.

I move in the other direction, spill out of the frame, snag my gold lamé dress on a nail protruding from the wall, punctuating a pale scar where a portrait used to hang. My biggest fear, my dress unraveling, my body exposed so dramatically that I'm rendered unrecognizable: slipping carelessly there and back again, using my own agitation and confusion to deceive her. Reversing her attention to the apple rotting on the windowsill as I despair over erasing all the hints and problems left to solve from this text. Brushing evidence onto the floor, sweeping it under the tablecloth; inserting a flashback as an alteration in the sequence of events.

There are innumerable ways of performing; I haven't done the things I should've done to keep her occupied, drowning in champagne, giving her time for frills and for herself, snatching a stop watch from the prop table. Demanding order and efficiency through constant repetition, transforming the life of my tenderfoot housewife until she's exhausted, taken to drink, reading popular fiction, sprouting cheap costume jewelry right out of her skin. Though she's disgracefully tattered, hocking the family silver in order to maintain the illusion of being well-to-do. Disguising herself, limbering around in literature as an insatiable woman, involving herself deeply in other's affairs.

The truth is that I made this all up. The truth is that I didn't want a story, I wanted something real for once. The curtain falls and she keeps on terrifying me, turning to moaning, not exactly what I was looking for. Her resemblance to a rejected woman is uncanny; she handles her wretchedness in the traditional way, putting on more and more makeup, translating her desire by making no effort to hide it, searching frantically for something to do with herself. After the dusting, sweeping, after the dishes are done and the bed made, the floor scrubbed and polished. She could be sustained entirely by her private life, the double meaning of everything she does, even those dull, repetitive things, which compel her to move on, believing in herself, hemming and hanging ruffles on every available surface. Anything to delay the shock of the truth, too many memories trailing behind.

Whatever comes by my window will be an encounter I can approach cautiously. I'm not quite sure, boys leaping over the backyard fence to save the daffodils from losing their heads early: I'm folding clothes, flustered by the static warmth of spring.

Making a pillowcase, a tablecloth, a picnic blanket into a form I can wear.

Waiting for the bus in the last slice of sunlight remaining between the bulk of two houses, shadows lounging over the street, snagging on the wheels of passing cars. I switch my face so the sun won't hit it and a boy screams *Bitch. Bitch what does it feel like to wear red lipstick,* holding out his hand.

My hand closing on the bell, this is my stop. Walking toward the front of the bus the doors split open, a crowd of teenage girls dressed in striped baseball uniforms surge then stop, falling back as I come forward. *She's so pretty,* one says.

Inside I slide my heel down against the slick floor, toe turned up. I roll my chewing gum between thumb and forefinger, press it against the bottom of my seat: a satisfying stick, then stuff my hand between the pages of a book to keep my place. A mirror on either side of me and behind a black velvet curtain. The curtain covers a stepladder hanging from two hooks, a ladder laid horizontally along the wall, impossible to climb. Confiding to two microphones, a tape recorder, what it feels like to wear red lipstick. Glistening with audible sounds, a hiss lisping on each solid S, lipsssstick. Red lipstick thrusting my tongue against my teeth making a sound, the sound of snails, the flickering of lips.

FOUR

I do things well. I do it wrong. I beg to stay where I'm clearly not wanted. I've plead too many intimate details, confessions too wild and intense to be endured.

I've been indulged by vague objects, unintended uses of doubles and duplicates.

With everything entirely out of sight, I'll continue to fall and fall again.

To hold on, I'll sensibly gather all that's not wanted. All there is of papers, clipped coupons, clusters of golden teeth – every little proof of beauty, and bring a large sheet of paper to wrap what I've made.

While folding an ample envelope, I see the lock of hair I'd once unconsciously curled round my finger. The lock I'd twisted the moment I firmly set upon my purpose. I'd wound this hair with no other emotion than a private and unrespectable love. A shriek almost escaped me as the curl vanishes beneath the paper I fold.

The packet I fasten with a ribbon, and a black seal bearing my impression.

I finish and say, *Here is a parcel. Will you throw it in when you pass over the mouth of the river.*

She looks at it for an instant and then at me. Her look can never be conceived.

I have become an inconvenience, I say.

The little home in the wood where I live is warm, and on the morning of her expected visit I dress myself in red and place a clock on a small table near shadows gathered without the window, where I'd spread a white tablecloth.

I wish you wouldn't, she says.

There is only one red letter left, the milk taste of ink, papers melting on my tongue.

I like to see what words will do, let them slide up to one another for a while. I force myself to get out of bed and change everything; all I've got is a few ladyposes and expressions to rework and revise. Why is it so yellow? What is she doing here? Sometimes, all of a sudden I misplace a semi-colon or replace myself with the third person, a woman cutting tangerines from a tree with a pair of gleaming shears. Or clementines: I'm not sure what the difference is.

She'll say, *Hi, do you want a bite of this tangerine?* And I'll bite it, and then I'll know. You know?

On the last days the horizon was so clear I could see routinely invisible islands striking an arresting silhouette over the sea. What keeps me from getting down into the water, a continuous wound of salt displacing every ship. No way out to sea but to swim, not sure of what I'm doing, lacking the stamina to continue. I'd like to get out there, remove the wedge of sand bracketing the bay, reverse the relationship. A woman sitting down to write, her fingers white with cold hovering over the keys.

What to say; I can't tell much more. I can't tell you how I see myself. I'm not sure of what I'm doing. If I leave out all the words what is left behind? Some residue, a soup of chalk and ink; women swimming laps like they can't stop, even though the water's cold, icy so it'd peel layers of skin right off like nail polish. All this blank space allows for anything to happen. Anything could happen, I take all I can get. I might become a total mess. I might create this messy manuscript, a text that escapes narrative through attention and exultation of the everyday. I recognize things here from my own life, which I've distorted in order to entertain somebody. I'd do this every day for hours on end if I could go on.

FIVE

The heat of light on my face has real warmth. If I turn too far I'm blinded. The light follows me from room to room. In my heels, I can see out the window of the next-room over, if I lift my head. I suffer from a kind of shyness in the camera's presence. The light blocks its motions in the room beyond, although I can hear the reel whirling in its case. I make an effort to keep the camera at a distance. Again and again, I shut the door.

The cat runs out into the snow and whips around, back in. She wants to be where I am, to know what I'm doing. I sit at the vanity, crescents swinging aimlessly from my earlobes. I can't sit still enough to make them stop. I don't wait to be told what to do, but when someone says the telephone is ringing I answer it and say *Hello?* although the film is silent. I want to laugh; there isn't anybody on the other end.

Cigarettes lined up like tattered crayons, half-smoked, and ruined by lipstick prints. The ache of unfilled gestures, a tension in my throat like crushed violets. If I happen to glance directly at the camera, I try to cover it up by looking quickly away, seeking out a place to settle. The mirror is safest; I can only see myself, it's like the camera isn't even here.

What I'm doing is easily forgotten. I started out by changing clothes. When I take my place, I'm infinitely enhanced. I am here, heightened by the light which startles me, moved to act by the camera which records the ordinary things I do: trimming my bangs, putting on lipstick and wiping it off, drinking tea. I hold the cat down with one hand and try to light another cigarette with the other. When the cat falls, I let her go. When the lighter will not light the cigarette, I'm disgusted, and throw them across the room. The film wasn't in the camera, so I have to do it again, for real this time, clicking the wheel on the lighter with my thumb, the cigarette damp in my mouth. Other girls walk in and out of the room. The small incidents of girls doing things will be disposed in an order, but until then they keep strutting back and forth; the house is built like a railroad. The girls want to know what they should do. Three minutes lasts forever; we often run out of the thing we're doing and continue to stand there, foolishly, trapped by a static whir, and the glaze of lights.

SIX

I'm often watching myself being looked at. Whenever I do anything, even a simple thing like washing the dishes, I see myself as willfully deceiving. I'm never only washing the dishes; there's inevitably another thing. I wash the dishes with the faucet losing a steady stream of lukewarm water; washing the dishes and suffering an anger that's turned into a way of pleasing. Both of these and the beauty of effective anger, a flush that comes without even trying. I'm constantly uncertain of what it is that I'm doing but likewise undeceived; I'm certainly not washing the dishes. The tawny yellow of the dish washing liquid is a serviceable color, diluted with water. I repeatedly return each dish to the dish rack, gloating over their cleanliness, the hygienic quality of dishes drying on the countertop, a vanity in the gleam of stacks of silverware. I refuse to be stopped by objections, I'll keep on cleaning, outraged by my own strength, scrubbing the stove with steel wool and vinegar. Each flaw I scrub activates my feelings of resentment. There's nothing I'd rather do but this. I do the floors as I please, the mop unpredictable, potentially monstrous. I bury my diamond in the laundry detergent, the click of my tongue emphasizing discontent. Glass shatters on tile and I sweep it neatly with a dustpan, crouching on my haunches, prepared to begin my disappearing act.

I'm puzzled by the house's behavior; baptized, it's no less humiliated. Maybe there's still something here for me to do, a thing I've been unable to move toward until I found a way to place the house in my authority. All day I've been making persistent and active attempts to stimulate a wholesome modesty, efforts at which I falter, my body fainting; with eager haste I gobble down a cup of coffee and start all over again. Absorbed and breathless, I seeks out bits of mold, specks of food that might be between this crevice, that altar. I might be stopped but

a woman must continually watch herself. I'm drawn to see the limitations of a filthy house as an opportunity for drawing blood.

SEVEN

If I look long enough, I'm confronted by her imperfections. What I'm looking for is a flaw, something not quite right: an offense against articulation, her limbs' position conveying a sense of unease. Her arms weak, swinging in their sockets, a blemish on her cheek: the result of a headfirst fall from the bookcase where she rests, supported by a wire stand. My impulse is to apologize for these mistakes, factory glitches she arrived with, stains that occurred as a work of my own authorship. The most infinitesimal scratch transformed to an unstoppable gash, serrating her body in two. This difference is ornamental; I can switch, right now, distract myself by covering her mouth with my thumb, buffing her forehead with a piece of white paper or cloth. A notion I don't like: I don't want to take the risk of ruining her further, taking her apart piece by piece, knocking her over, sending her bits flying across the floor, where the cat will take up one posable leg, feline incisors grinding against it like an eraser head. The unfortunate problem of her plastic eyes under the couch, looking in opposite directions. Things I don't have control over put me on edge; I can't stop noticing that her deficiencies disappear and reappear as I look toward and away, going over her line by line. Things that take time to do: measuring the distance between her eyes and the wedge of her nose is all I need to get there, counting the hairs in each plug on her scalp. It doesn't matter, there is always a resistance: the fabric of her dress will tear, she will dirty her feet, fall off-balance and break off her ear lobe. Her eyelashes will fall out and litter the floor like pine needles. Her blush will wash away at my glance. I tried to take care of her; I tried to preserve her original state, but not as well as I thought. She sounds out each of her deformities in her own language, claiming them as her personal accomplishments. Composed but not confining: a blank space where her lipstick should be, a tiny hole at the back of her knee, the broken spring inside her head, harmonies that are dear to her. She will substitute frizzy hair and a cracked behind for glamour, creating a correspondence between beauty and irregularity that I can put a value to. Her approach is brutal, simple: she is sure of herself, opening and closing her eyes as a trigger for serenity.

EIGHT

I carry my own mattress around with me. Beautiful daughters of the wood, treading ground carpeted with downy pine needles. The deafening noise of girls passing between beauty and death. I'd flown to the river, dropped my handkerchief on a shrub near the shore. Wading into the water in my heavy black dress, waves darkened with roses. The rumble of girls gossiping, while I prepare to hide myself, my hair floating on the surface of the water.

I can't keep up. I can't be entirely preserved from insects; they'll stride around me, stoke me. I'd held a lantern burning on the pure spirit of sugar cane, left it perched on a rock interceding on water. The river moves me forward, away from my last light. My skirt rises like hair, my body stripped, pendulous, dangling in the water below the deflated balloon of my woolen dress.

Girls patrol the banks, hesitating at each inlet. A girl says, *She must have put it somewhere I haven't looked yet.* Girls need time to collect. Girls need to look tenderly, with warmth and regret. They come after me and find I'm steadily shrinking.

They take me out of the water and dry me off. I've shriveled up a little but will soon fill out. They put a necklace around my neck like they are choking me, as if each stone in the circlet were their fists all wrapped around. I have to let all these things happen.

I pick up my mattress and head back to the wood, a galaxy of girls sparking around me. One says, *Take that thing off and come here.*

My bright, hard *No*, afraid my voice will break. I lean into the wood, biting my lip, withdrawing into a cluster of trees. I haven't done enough to fulfill my hopes. I mean to keep my distance.

But I cut out a doll for her, a girl says, *without scissors*. The doll could be a substitute for me. The girls take the doll and caress it; they comb its hair and clinically observe the weight of ink in a doll made of paper. A girl says, *She has flaws*, touching the doll's knee, folding the paper so that the doll can walk. A paper doll made flexible, capable of moving. *I mean to have this monster chronicled*, a girl says, watching the doll follow her into the forest. A girl plucks another doll from a sheet and lets it fall.

Hordes of disagreeable girls roam the woods, carrying lanterns mantled with candy. The cloths that should have covered their faces they leave waving from the limbs of trees. A system of constraint holds them together, corrupts their bodies. They pull themselves together, using each other to find a way. They have something; they take each one by the hand. They look up and they watch the moon rising on water. Girls imitating each other and not succeeding, changing a little each time until the imitation is unrecognizable.

I fold into my palm a fistful of stones. Perched on the edge of the wood I throw each stone into the water. I call out names and nearly every name is wrong. I ask what they would do if I came in white and no one else was wearing white? Would they say that I am wrong? I want a kind of excess, a signal.

Striking the forest floor, I feel I will ignite a wildfire, a girl that leaves a black smudge behind.

NINE

I stand behind the camera, looking through the spectacle. If I can suspend myself, I can catch them going by, and I will keep them. Starting too soon, two girls ride by, long hair rippling to the very last strand, accurately reproduced. At a distance, and then near enough to force into movement. Close enough, far too close to know. They are there, held here within the space allowed, and then out. Drawn forward and then back, they circle round, and return. I move between looking through and lifting. They stop when I say, *Now*, where I want them to be. Dropping their heels from the pedals. Passing cars cut them off entirely.

I can't tell what the film is doing inside the cartridge, it's inscrutable; it offers nothing — there is no way to go back and see what's happened, rewind, reply. Not a productive moment, or was it a long pause. So I have her do it over again, and again, hoping that this time I've got something. She thought she'd seen my mistake and asked me, so I told her. I held the button down. Was it long enough? If an image has been recorded, it's an image in which she speaks, but no sound remains to be released. Her mouth moving, and the image continues. I can't capture the brilliant, hard and real red of her mouth, or the sound of her body moving forward in the folding chair as she leans in, pushing handfuls of hairpins around on a sheet of paper.

I put a mark on the film and run the camera for a second. The mark disappears; this is what is happening. A tape is winding, a flimsy ribbon. A girl selected and searched, on and off her bicycle, soaking paper in a dish of cold water. The danger is that I might not stop.

TEN

It isn't only a girl.

Not only the light that's brought her forward, ready to smile. The switch from gold – fabric gathers, her throat buttoned closed with pearls. Two girls need to learn to share. I want everything for myself, a pinafore, a barrette to hold back this falling forward lock of hair. Everything she has might as well be mine. Her throat closed up by a seam, her split: a whisper then a roar. I only ever see her: she takes up all the space. Her hands moving across typewriter keys like spiders building a web, swinging back on forth, hitting shift.

Everything is arranged so that she can see what I can't: I want her perspective, to switch sides so I can look, eavesdrop on the images she has access to. Red flowers bursting open, a girl scratching a pencil across a sheet of blue veined paper. Light but certain. She doesn't go all the way off. Two red notes on sheet music: her finger pricked by a scissor point. Swearing with her heart, her hand. Wiping the scissor blade clean on the edge of a table. Pulling her knee socks up. Insects throbbing in crayon boxes. Collecting what she needs: cupping her hand against a sun warmed wall to scoop a lizard into a bucket. A bucket of lizards with their tails snapped off. *I only need the tails*, she says. A line of ordered trees leaning in the wind so that the smaller rests on the taller. Her skirt brushing back against her knees, her bucket swinging from her elbow. She goes up and down the stairs, coming back carrying everything she owns. Every belonging has its own box, and a new paragraph must begin.

A household loaded with little girls. Mending her smile with a tube a lipstick. She presses and color floods. The steam from a teakettle rises into her hair as she pours. The cat looks up at once, anxious for a spilt drop of cream. She does it again, pouring the water more dramatically this time, her elbow lifted away from her body, jutting out at an angle. The cat's gone on; she did something wrong the first time around. With each retake her hair contracts, coils, hisses and splits. I recharge the batteries, she bites her fingernails, spitting jagged half-moons into my teacup. She wouldn't do this if it couldn't be on film. If she did not do this, I wouldn't be watching her, making each moment into an acquisition.

I'd rather have a situation than a household. In relation to my surroundings, I feel very small. I was putting on my lipstick when I was stopped. She called me a sulking girl. I managed my lower lip quite well; it barely trembled. She said the place I was in would be better occupied by somebody else. Someone dressed in decent blue, not sullen, thin pink with stained fingertips, lacquered green. I rolled back an empty sound, one slip strap creeping down my bare shoulder. I couldn't confirm whether she was right or not but I had to do something. I unfurled myself from my cramped position like a hermit crab coming out of its shell to trundle along the beach. I'd rather live in an empty soda can or a perfume bottle. I snatched every dress from my closet and tossed them upon the floor. I'm bound to recklessness, tenderness.

You asshole, I murmured, tossing cheap paperback romances through the air. They moved around us like moths, women mourning before cold grey mansions, long dresses sought by the wind and waves. Women brooding over their budget books.

A light touch is needed. Limpid gliding hours, a forest hung with slender limbs and one visible absence I can long after. The moon startled from its canopy, bouncing on treetops as if on a mattress. The moon, small and restless, flirting with the daylight. It's unlikely I'd ever ride a bicycle. I'm not the kind of girl to carry a sewing kit in my coat pocket.

I don't associate myself from here. I like to think of the beautifully ordinary; unmendable garments, tea soaked in ounces of honey, the filmy brilliance of face powder dusting the cover of a magazine – untidiness and lavender stink. She's been overcome by my efforts, the mild sins of a shabby little girl, toting home stray dressers, wobbly chairs. A slow, soothing accrual of stuff, the unbearable heat of things sidling up to me, wearing me out. The small affairs of the coffee table and the bookcase.

She tapes a dictionary to the window frame to still its rattling.

ELEVEN

Here's what happens when I let myself go: it never works. I keep coming back to the same thing; I'm distracted by the terrible shape of women with their heads held in their hands. They make unsteady, awkward triangles; they make me uncomfortable. I get anxious and then I start to dump girls in like goldfish. They slither into place, some wearing party hats and shooting off their mouths. I want to untangle them by cutting every knot.

Each outfit guaranteed by matching earrings: it's right like this. More elaborate, lightweight, both swift and well. The smooth margin of one girl's cheekbone, swooping into a blustering wave. How did she get in here, what is she doing now, eavesdropping on the neighbors? Moving her to a different space does nothing: she still looks and acts the same as she did surrounded by all those rhododendrons.

The visual question of her smile, put out and then carried away.

I should be able to fit as many girls as I need in here, cram them alongside stray buttons, hooks and eyes, velvet millinery flowers, aged satin ribbon, tweezers, Vaseline and handkerchiefs. All the girls will come wearing pastel party frocks, carrying presents wrapped in tin foil. I should be able to get as many girls as I need. In here, there's room for them all; a dressing room for every girl, a looking-glass to empty out the embryos of a thousand pimples. The radiant lustre of girls full sweet and dainty.

TWELVE

My accumulated dresses may be carved out of hard candy. Glossy, almost perfect; I want to lick them. The enunciation of silk, satin and velvet, crushed in the closet: a creeping grammar. If only I didn't have to give anything back; I'd finally be able to do what I might do if I had everything I wanted. Time might be taken by a repertoire of poses, unmendable gestures mingling with frail beasts. The velocity of motion determined by a pinked hem.

Fur must never overact, must be reconciled to passively lying still, like a tuna fish. If I place myself on a park bench, little birds come and rest on my hat. Impulsive birds pausing for a moment, flaunting the splendor of their out-turned wings. In the moments before young girls are thrilled, walking by. A tiny bird lifting off my hat, dissolving in the light of a noonday sun.

Nothing ever stands still, nothing ever breaks. I can continue as before, seeking out each serge and seam. These details may betray, may serve as evidence of expressions of the body, a substitute for speech. My initials embroidered in the lining of my kidskin gloves; the special knowledge of thread pulsing against an artery. A charm produced and sustained by this small addition, by the silk crepe lining of my wool coat, the extra layers of lace in my petticoat. Every morning I constitute myself: a wide toothed comb, a makeup brush kept clean with witch hazel. The dishes won't get done, not in time, not tomorrow. A thin film of blue-grey mold unfolds itself over the top of yesterday's coffee, lurks in the bottom of a cup. The inconvenience of every cup that needs me. They may never be completely satisfied, but at least my apron looks cheerful, hanging from a hook on the back of the door. The efficiency of an apron is hard to bear, but familiar. I have no need to mop the floor or iron the tablecloth as long as the apron is there. There is a pleasure in movement and a variety of things to be done; I need to find a way to keep my stockings from sliding down around my ankles. It puts me in a mood for cake and failure. Speak clearly, skirt, sashay. Every possible daytime occasion may be included here; this is a story told by the dress I wear, no different from my skin.

THIRTEEN

A samovar, a sink. In regular succession or promiscuously; the misery of all at once. A hot flush, a headache and bruised knees. A bouquet on every branch bending toward the street, girls in borrowed garters dropping press-on nails in the stairwell like blossoms, silvery-pink and fluttering. I'm inclined to collect them all, the nails of generous women clogging every gutter. The bottoms of my shoes crusted with yellow blooms like snot. Great pink clumps surging, as if a cord has been pulled, a shade opened, a door and her eyelid.

A salt rain in the clouds, the scent of kelp and whales with mouths ringed with ancient toothbrush bristles, caught in loaded trees, shaking salt to the street. Velvet surging, all too much at once, my heart struggling against my stomach. The house won't hold.

Pushing a sponge-headed mop over the floorboards in an effort opposite the direction of the boards laid across the room. Swallowing when I'm done, slowly and clearly. I keep myself busy by holding onto something. It is still raining and the rain has nothing to do but sink.

A welt carved into my thigh from an object which I kept on my lap for a while but which is now gone.

Street signs and addresses wavering, as if cold, water riveted to broken doorbells, no call to fetch me from suffering. Herds of trees anticipating the mail: no packages today. A rupture in the sky and the streetlights struggle to turn on, hissing and buzzing like bawling girls, pulling pigtails. If this continues, I'll learn to swim: a bucket and a bathtub, a girl in galoshes with a broom, sweeping tadpoles toward the drain, taking care to catch each one. For no reason but a way of keeping time: each stroke, feet together, knees together, blowing out air. Can I count each button, every light I left on, a room I don't use?

A door left slightly open, so that the cat hurdles against it, his claws catching on the bottom edge of the frame: he pulls and pulls, the force of one cat wanting in, battling a block of wood. When it swings open, he falls back, legs pumping and then thrusting forward, propelling himself from floor to window ledge. The screen he can't get by bounces him back. He moves in the way of girls jumping rope, hula-hoops, somersaults.

The heartlessness of silver lined hips. Hard to get salt water out of silk. I'd wear black before a tragedy, inexplicably snap a button from my sleeve with my teeth. Swallowing a whole suit's worth of small buttons, glutted in my belly; the sound of buttons shuffling against each other in the bottom of a girl. My dress punctuating me, coming to a full stop at my wrist, resting on a sleeve. Kneecaps scarcely seen, hovering beyond the outermost edge of my slip. I depend upon a breeze to start unsettling the arrangement of my skirt; otherwise, I'll have to start making unrestricted movements, crackling in chiffon. The extra charge of glamour distilled by the telephone's ring; when I answer my obligations the illusion is effaced – I answer as anybody might, the receiver clinging to an anxious ear, the trunk wafting through my loose, dismantled hair. The threat of fabric, simulating skin; I take time to slouch in satin, taming my dress to bargain, blackmail, bless. I'm clashing with the scenery, collar slightly askew – a girl groomed by tulle, raiding the dress rack. I'm always stopping here, stooping to see myself set loose by the earth. Mountains around me peeling, shedding slate.

To be the prettiest, the most ready to descend. From the rituals of the jungle gym to nylon stockings stretched over wire hangers. The forest is empty of anything but girls in white dresses. They can do what they like, such as slip into a clock. They don't like to be told what to do, to have the mechanics explained. Time is often passing and what they love is to steep in the senselessness of forest paths lit by fluorescent lights; the feel of a kidskin glove on a bare thigh; the limpid eye of a rose in her lap. If I leave, I can go anywhere: from here to a seesaw, a swing, a shallow swimming pool. Because I have been alone and I have flung myself from here, drawn by the constant gravity of trains moving underground, the incessant pull of water to the sea. Girls in a city they've never seen, every tree a furnace for forgetting.

A kind of maze of white ankle socks. The kinds of snakeskin secrets girls have, sloppily abandoned in favor of something new. I haven't told anyone; I've been hushed by moths wrapped in wax paper and the relentless ache of getting ready to be in line. Moving forward to smile, to lift my chin so the bones in my neck collapse.

A girl won't ever be here again. She'll lose some blood, cut her nails, her hair – but no wound. And then again, the bathtub water lukewarm, clogged with skin cells, soap.

Fourteen

Carrying on without caring which way I'm going. To the left, an eggshell with a light bulb popped on inside, fluorescence blooming. To the right, the luxury of a household without the fixative of a line. I go forward; I've been learning language, what a pen can show. Putting this together, falsifying and fabricating as I go along: the privilege of fiction to adapt abruptly, disregard mysteriously opened doors. Relying on rupture to cause my downcast face to lift up in excitement.

The word and the image forced apart, adjusting to accommodate the body of a girl between spacer and lead. The pressured glances that act against her, pinning her to a window frame, her skirt spread. I've been doing less than nothing, like a mannequin turning round, exhibiting the sediment of all this glitz, voluptuous gauze heaving gracelessly, incapable of responding to a breath. Scrutinized for the light I spill, wastefully. I'm often longing to save these stars, toxic to touch, lethal to look at directly. To lose myself I've provoked particular encounters, changed direction, adapted the text to allow in the possibilities rising before me. The exemplary force of what I can't see without looking; flocks of seashells erupting in my garden, crushing every sprout. The beauty and the blemish of a girl caught in a series of self-reflections, turning towards delicate little objects to balance out her unmistakable eyes. The delicious and satisfying accumulation of so much stuff: I want to cultivate a galaxy. The backdrop of secondary pleasures, functionally endless: the illusion of a sky at the end of an alleyway, clouds on cardboard. The difference cannot be blocked from view.

She can be said to speak. To speak back as a symptom of her of her reflection. To speak back after swallowing an egg from its shell as a manner of taking sustenance while exhausted by emotion. What she says, if I acknowledge hearing it, is yes. To whatever happens, whatever surplus I invent: yes and yes, demanding yes and suggesting yes and contributing her yes as a prelude to action. Latching onto the camera, wearing the lens as a mask: yes, she says.

If I am prepared to live, I will not be indifferent; I will listen and readily reply. I will not hesitate to call.

Fifteen

Long hair mangled by the sun's soft focus, flustered strands stuck to her painted lips. Copper kisses for charcoal eyes, a bird batting against a lace curtain, the wind pushing back her dress so that she sparks, flares. The rooted color of her eyes, singed at the edge; tipping back her face comes closed. The envelope in her apron pocket, stamp canceled, slit open with a kitchen knife. The letter inside read with a magnifying glass, a pinpoint of light setting it to flame.

Her hair now neatly noosed, not a single strand escaping from the tight braid pressed between her shoulder blades. Otherwise, hair slipping forward, soaking in her teacup. Little beauty for herself, her dress hung upon the wall like a painting, nobody inside; all she needs is a white dress thrown across her back like a fox's pelt, split in the middle with the sleeves sticking out, starched. She'll make it look effortless and natural. She might even be pleased by a piece of chocolate wrapped in pink foil, unpeeling it a work she can do with her hands: the foil in one piece. She can look now, cautiously from the doorway: holding out her long hair to be combed and rolled at the nape of her neck, a plump coiled garden snail suckling her skull.

A deep breath and not a word; all the cleaning she's done uncontrollable, unraveling itself, a dust that won't stop coming to rest. Every line she ever said she said herself: *All women or only beautiful women?* She started with the first words and kept on. Transfixed by light and by its destructive power. Neurotically smoothing down the long plaits of her hair, her hands knuckled, creeping up and down; she can't stop touching herself, her rings glinting in ways she can't see. Doing all this by hand, each infinitesimal thing decided by her, made by her, brought here by her; an obsession that goes beyond recreating, a kind of resistance offered by her dress, doing what a body can't. A way of distracting, coming in and out of focus with each indrawn gasp; a tangerine pulsing in a dish, the visible distance of her hair overwhelming, sprung from her head like thunder.

A fleeting glimpse of a positive image: I can't make out her face. A girl pressed and dried like a photograph, between the pages of this book. A bad transfer, skin squealing as the camera pans from left to right, from floor to ceiling, from head to toe. A girl encased in mirrors, on her own in the most public manner possible. A girl revolving without division between the wall and the floor, performing the most menial, degrading and frivolous chores. Visuals detached from a narrative like untethered moons. No planet to see by, the bluish skin tone of a girl lost in blooming over the surface, thousands of rampaging beauties moving inexorably towards a strange but real brilliance.

Equipped with paper and tulle, sheets, handkerchiefs and safety pins. What can I do with these things that will make it possible to go on; how should I arrange them? What will come first? A star projecting allure, ignoring totally her radiant transformation. There's not much here but damp hair, distilled flowers. How to hold her lovely confidence, losing not one single drop; how to hold her breath, how to make a ritual to bring her back, slowly, advancing with her feet turned out, so that I can see her coming. The area just beyond her face gorged with glass, color and light. A distance that leaves me cold, without fixed hours, longing to be less far from pleasure. I would have liked exactly the opposite. The leaking bellows of waist high windows, a girl lovingly reproduced so that she might have the chance to overcome crude lighting, unbearably clumsy exaggerations: yes, tinsel and stardust, and cellophane, too.

A headache band of beauty round her temple, drawn too tight. She's too often been betrayed and continued dancing through the night. She's posed to the best of her ability, taken the elaborate preparations necessary to greet the light: an ermine filched from a cupboard, a scraggly slip wafting to her ankles. What is doing and what is undone? She's gone aside to the water, to the river and committed herself to the sea.

As she leaves the house, she sets things in order: the sterling sorted, linens starched and pressed. A drop cloth thrown over every mirror, a bereavement of beauty and the light goes out.

I'm seldom able to remain still; I come forward, faintly emerging from the background. It's so hard to keep still while I have so much to do. I've been caught in a change, obliged to put on charmeuse silk, restored to powdering my face without the aid of artificial light.

A cat can call for her dinner, at the window cawing, attempting to come in clearly. If the phone rings, I won't answer; I'll bend back the lid of this cat food can with a butter knife, mashing cold, soft meat into a dish. Hold open the window with an upended book, spine wedged against the screen. My hand coveting a clamshell, the business of domestic life fulfilling every moment with soapsuds. She's been abandoned in her dress too long, mopping spilt tea. Guided by my feeling like embroidery thread pulled through a tapestry by a tiny needle. Only so small, only like this. And then, and before, but especially after: the duties of the house, sweetly humiliating; doing this on my hands and knees, pleased to be pointing out every error. Why am I not yet done? This is a thing I need to do, which must be done, which will never be finished, page by page. A part of every day is given, and cannot be had back: not for anything, not for the relics of winter, not for the heavy lock of hair falling forward onto her face. The terror of not knowing what will come next, what will the next thing be. Have I revealed her poorly, hip thrust forward, one toe pointed at the camera like a machine gun?

Only persistence and patience, a cardinal on my ring finger, a dappled deep-eyed deer in a haze of incandescent light.

.

ABOUT THE AUTHOR

Roxanne Carter received her MFA in Literary Arts from Brown University in 2008, and a Ph.D. in Creative Writing from the University of Denver in 2011. Her work has appeared in *Tarpaulin Sky, Fact-Simile, Drunken Boat, La Petite Zine,* and *Sidebrow* among others. She lives in Ohio, where she blogs at www.persephassa.com